CW00493716

## About the Author

A stint as a police constable in the Kent County Constabulary. Then moved onto the army. I have been a soldier with two tours of Northern Ireland.

Most of my working life, I have been a warehouse man. Now I look after my wife. But I do have a story or two to tell, for those that want to listen.

# Nefatia, Goddess of the Lahmian Sisterhood

**Paul Tuley**

# Nefatia, Goddess of the Lahmian Sisterhood

Olympia Publishers
*London*

**www.olympiapublishers.com**
OLYMPIA PAPERBACK EDITION



A CIP catalogue record for this title is
available from the British Library.

ISBN: 978-1-84897-900-0



First Published in 2018

Olympia Publishers
60 Cannon Street
London
EC4N 6NP

Printed in Great Britain

# CHAPTER ONE

Bosco de Warley, Rutland, England 1290. The fat bishops sit in their palaces of gold, eating the perfectly cooked side of beef. Romping, fornicating with the ladies of the local gentry, in all their finery. The King and his court imbibe the finest wines and mead and ales, and gorge on the finest venison and suckling pig. They are entertained by the jester, the court acrobats and the bear baiter before the king goes to his bedchamber, to make love to his queen.

The farmer, ploughman, wheelwright, fletcher, cooper, all wending their way home, after a long day in the field plying their trade. Back to their hovel, looking forward to a hot meal of barley broth, along with the freshly made maslin. Followed by a good night's sleep. But just like the Bishop and King, not knowing if they would survive the night, to see the bright dawning of a new day.

A country that was an open sewer, a cesspit! As well as being the highway for pedestrian traffic. The byways close cluttered streets and narrow passages; were the contours for every type of waste that everyone wanted to discard. The brooks, streams and rivers awash with animal as well as human waste.

A clean green country, the last thing on anyone's mind; complete disregard. Fifty percent of his wealth going to the vulgar, over-rich church, his landlord. Not caring about his tenants, as long as they paid their rent, so it could be added to the swelling coffers of the extortionate church. At a time, when the church had scant regard for its priests or parishioners. Hypocrisy, extortion, resentment, greed, power ran amok. It was always the poor that paid the price, suffering in the end. The Holy Roman Empire disguising itself as the Catholic Church! It was never as holy as when with its papal and bull decrees; it extorted money. If it could not gain the power and wealth it wanted it would resort to sending in its own army to kill its own faithful. To usurp the power that held the country in a stable condition. All to increase the sway and influence the church had over its minions. That was the only consideration of the overweight clergy, at this time. The other fifty percent went to his liege the king as tax. So he has very little to spare for his family and himself. So as an individual he has little care about his own existence. The population a scant two million at most. Ravaged by poor diet, insanitary conditions. Which in the end gave way to typhoid, dysentery, diphtheria and smallpox.

Myself, I can only ever remember being on my own, fending for myself. Cast off at some stage by my parents, as an encumbrance I assume. Unable to feed me, obviously not planned; a wretch to all concerned. Dumped in a small cavern, left to survive in this cold, wet corner, for I do not know how long. Something started sniffing me, licking me. Then pulling me, tugging me into the deep, dark recess at the back of the cavern. Putting me in the middle of the cluster of her three pups. Curling her furry body around all of us, she protected her cubs from the inclement weather. It felt so much better to be part of something than being left alone to protect myself, from whatever waited for me, in this dark diseased place.

In the morning the wind whistled at the mouth of the cavern. Mother had already gone out to eat. No doubt she had feasted on rats again. On her return, I crawled over to her; to feed from her nipples that she offered to me. My three brothers did not seem interested at all. After filling myself on her thick white milk, she ventured off to the furry young bodies. Her muzzle pushing, then turning; but they were lifeless. No longer with us, dead taken by the plague. My mother the she-wolf looked after me. She did not stint on attention, motherly love, feeding; but most importantly she taught me the craft of survival. In this godforsaken land. She kept me warm at night, kept me hidden away during the day. When she felt I was big enough, that was the first time she took me out into the vast open spaces of Rutland. I rode on her back for a short while. If she got annoyed with me, she would pull me back by gripping my ankle and let go. The first time doing this, she gripped too tight. Penetrating my weak skin with her sharp fangs, making me bleed. Her saliva running over the small open wound, probably giving me her lupus albus virus. Especially, as she was an albino wolf. But it was for my own good after all. Plus it did no real damage to me. As I grew, my mother started to show her age. So it was me that became the hunter. It was me that fed my mother. It was me that tended her wounds, keeping her clean. It was me that kept her warm at night, by holding her tight to my young body. Our hearts beat as one, my body warmth keeping her safe and secure from anyone that might want to finish her. It was me that chewed her food, when she could not do it herself.

My biggest kill was a very young roe deer. I snuffed out its life by jumping on its back then pushing my fingers in against its throat. Then, as it fell to the ground, I held its mouth closed, my other hand over its nose, just stifling it. Dragging it back to our cave, it lasted some few days. But I could feel my mother's life force slowly ebbing away. So we made the most of our feast; I kept her warm at night. During the day, I sat with her head in my lap, talking to her. Remembering the good times together, as mother and son. Then finally her eyes closed, never to re-open. Her final breath passed between her teeth and lips. I sat howling at the moon, with a sense of loss and loneliness. I pined for her to return, nudging her, but there was no life there. I sat there, struggling with what to do next. I had known her all my life, now I had to carry on without her. My life was in my hands.

As I had not eaten for such a long time, not wanting to be separated from the only parent I ever knew. I ripped apart the she-wolf, ravenous she fed me fully for the next three days. Now as one with the she-wolf the lupus albus was within me. Always there to guide me, keep me safe, like she had done all her life. Sated, I felt it was time to venture out once again. I keep close to the forest, so that no one could see me. Skirting all the dwellings, I come across a lonely barn and homestead. There was no sign of life anywhere, so I went inside amongst the old straw and hay, then bedding myself down for the night in the darkest corner I could find.

# CHAPTER TWO

I awake half way through the day. The wind howls and whistles as it dances through, across this dilapidated structure. As I rise, I sense someone else is within the run-down building. Too late! They have seen me.

"Good gracious what have we here? A young boy, no clothes and I do not think he has seen the likes of me, ever in his life." She approached me, not sure what to do, I stood still. She smells very similar to my mother, but looks very different. Then she cries out in alarm as a scallion of rats surround her. Sensing her terror, I wade into the ferocious-looking vermin, killing half the brood, unable to catch the rest as they flee.

"My goodness young man, that was very impressive. Even quicker than my cat. Come, follow me and let me feed you."

I did not understand a word she was saying. I could only converse in wolf, so I tried to show her I was hungry, by eating one of the rats!

She stood there, shaking her head.

"I am not sure where you have been, but you should have at least cooked the rat first."

The woman stood there, offering her hand to me. I went forward, putting my head against her hand. She rubbed my shaggy mane of hair, and then pointed to my hand. She took it into hers, as we walked towards her dimly lit house. I am sure she noticed that I was unkempt, my nails more like claws, pointed, sharp. My head forever looking around me, my eyes keen and body tense. I dare not relax.

"First you can eat. Then perhaps I will keep you, teach a little before you wander back to the wilds of Bosco de Warley. But if you want to stay longer, you are more than welcome."

I feel quite at ease, eating here. I do not feel the slightest bit threatened. As the woman talks to me, I point at my mouth, shaking my head. Then point to my ears, doing exactly the same.

"You respond to my words, but do not understand. I know who can help. My daughter Avicia can teach you the little she knows, so at least we can talk to each other. Wait until she comes back from the well. Perhaps you can help us along the way, in return."

I nod my head, baying, trying to smile; a sign of gratitude. The sign of acceptance I learnt from my mother. I go outside in the chilled afternoon, searching for anything to bide my time. I run off to the surrounding forest, downwind, as I hear something in there. There is a grunting or snuffling around a little deeper inside. I follow the noise until, there in front of me, I see a brood of wild boar piglets. Before they know what has happened, I have two of them. Broken necks, over my shoulder, then away; back to the homestead. I wait by the door, sat on my haunches, skinning the carcasses, with my long nimble nails and very defined-razor sharp teeth.

As the older woman comes out of the door, she nearly trips over me. "I thought you had gone. What have we here? Wild boar, skinned and ready. You are going to be useful, my boy. Avicia, come here! He has not left us. We have meat for at least two days thanks to him."

Avicia, the young ebony hued daughter with brown eyes, thick, long black hair looks at him as he tries to outstare her, but fails to do so.

"Mum, he looks like a wild young boy. I am sure he will learn, I love his vivid blue eyes. That mane of hair, he does not look human at all, does he?"

"He is possessed by something very strong. But while he is happy here, we will get along just fine. We do not have much, but it will be a pleasure, to have a man about the house again. If he brings meat like this to the table, then it will be no hardship sharing."

"Mum, we will have to be careful, that the sheriff does not discover the meat."

"That could be a problem. We will have to salt it, to cover the smell. Hide it from prying eyes, in the barn."

The girl comes over to me. Taking my hand, she leads me to the barn. I look over my shoulder, seeing the older woman taking the boar skins round the back of her home.

The two skinned pigs are covered in salt before being secreted away in the darkest corner of the barn. Then she comes to sit next to me, her hand tapping herself, "I am Avicia. A V IC IA. You try"

"AAAA."

"AV."

"AAA VV."

"Try to put them together, AV."

"AV."

All the time I am trying to say the word, she quietly pronounces the word for me to follow. I listen to the sound, the noise she makes. How she uses her lips. She smiles, her eyes lit up, giggling, as I try to make the same sound she does.

Determined not to be beaten I stand up, looking deep into her eyes, "Avicia, Avicia, AAAAVVVIIICCCIIIAAA," I howl with all my might.

"That is very clever. Now a name for you, something easy. Paen."

"You Paen, Paen, Paen. P… A… E… N, Paen."

Again as I try to pronounce this new word, which sounds so easy when Avicia says it to me, she quietly repeats it in the background.

"Pa… en. Paen, Paen, Paen."

I point to myself, baying at the top of my voice.

"Paen," I say. Then, hugging the young girl, my eyes wide, wild joyful, "Avicia, Avicia, Paen, Paen."

"Good, very good. Now we go home. But first can you say Mum? Just put your lips together, and then copy me. M… U… M…"

"Mum, Mum, Mum." Now I take Avicia by the hand; across the meadow, I had seen them earlier. Now I wanted to show her my skills. I left her laying in the grass. I lay down as low as I could get. Sliding along on my stomach, the scent made my nose itch in anticipation of the kill.

They did not see me until it was too late! A brace of hares, one in each hand. I stood up in the grass.

"Avicia, Avicia!"

She stood up smiling, jumping up and down with such glee. Then with a twist of their necks, their lives thwarted, gone in a flash. I give both the furry carcasses to her, she holds them close, as we walk back to the dwelling. That now, for the time being, seems to be my home. On arrival, Avicia rushes forward, the two hares held high as trophies.

“Look Mum, two hares to jug. So fresh, just a snap of their necks and they were done.”

I step forward, taking the two bodies. Then in front of them both, I show how I skin them with my nails and teeth. Skinned, gutted clean all in a matter of minutes. I look at the elder woman:

“Mum.”

I point at the younger girl, “Avicia,” then standing proudly, defiantly, my hand beating on my chest:

“Paen, Paen.”

“Well Avicia, you have been busy, so our young man can speak. As well as hares to be jugged. I have cut some of the boar, for a stew. Take Paen, collect some vegetables to go with the meat.”

Avicia guides me beyond their farmhouse, showing me their smallholding, which they cultivate as much as they can. We pick potatoes, turnip and beans for our meal.

As we sit together, the three of us around the hearth keeping warm, watching the food cook. I sit gnawing on a raw turnip, still unable to comprehend why the food needs to be hot. Why not just eat it as it is, like I have always done? Sate your hunger immediately. The woman and the girl talk. First, of the hardships of keeping on top of the farm work. Such a stroke of luck, my turning up as I did, into their quiet, ordinary lives. How perhaps, with a little training, they could get me to help them with physical work required to keep the farm alive. Rather than see them both become impecunious, bestowing on them a dissipation. Thus annulling mothers’ warrant of ownership, for not affording the tax due to the King. If they cannot secure the tenure of the land then they will be homeless, in this dark dismal plane of existence.

They both come round to look at me. I am weathered; I have a long mane of hair, which has never been cut. I am lean of body, hard with long nails, formed by my former life with the she-wolf. I have sharp, long incisors, due to eating raw meat to pulling the fur off the dead bodies and ripping shards of meat from our kills, all from my former life. Hard work will never kill me. They both smile as they feel my muscles, look at my hardened feet, toenails looking more like the claws of a dog. I have never needed what they call clothes, my hair keeps me warm.

"Avicia, I think tomorrow we will take him to the fields, show him the work and see how he finds it. He seems quite happy to do the hunting, so that will save us too. The skins are so clean, we can make use of those, for our bedding, amongst other things."

They both sit down again, giving me a bowl of their stew. Now it is hot, it does taste so completely different. But I still think I enjoy eating the way I have always taken my food; raw, still tasting the warmth of the body juices fresh after the kill.

# CHAPTER THREE

I still sleep in the barn, because I feel more at home there. Alone and from prying eyes. Also, should any old vagabond or miscreant attempt to rob or steal from the two women, I will be out here to reinforce the security of the whole farmstead. I have been farming now, for quite a while. Quite enjoy it too. I have developed into quite a powerful young man, even if I do say so myself. It is still only the two women that know about me. I keep away from strangers, only work when no one else is around, mainly during the night. My vision is so sensitive, I can see everything I need. I can hear the slightest noise. I still have not bothered with clothes, so I work tilling, ploughing the fields, with my one-man plough as naked as the day I was born. There is no pressure with the two women; Mum is a little older, she no longer works in the fields. Avicia is still active when she needs to be, but leaves all the heavy work to me. But sometimes I feel a little strange. I have a sudden urge to race across the fields, but not on my two legs; but on all fours to howl at the moon. During the day, I feel feverish and all of a sudden, I am on the floor, standing like a wolf, washing myself with my long, coarse tongue. My whole body covered from head to toe in fur, in silvery grey from head to toe. This is the time I need to go to the woods, to hunt, to kill something, anything just to satisfy this urge I have within me.

I lope into the forest, which takes me no time at all. I stop to smell the air. To the west I run unable to stop, or help myself. There I find a well-stocked farm. Find a young lamb, too easy to resist. Before I know it, I have clamped my jaw around its throat, taken its life. Then I am running from the enclosure, taking my kill with me. Retracing my steps, I stop to wash myself in the stream. Looking down I see myself, as a wolf, not a young man; covered in the blood of the lamb I just slaughtered. Having washed the corpse and myself, I think of the quickest way home. Once again I look into the sparkling water, seeing this time a lean, mean, very large and aggressive wolf. I lope off into the forest so as not to be seen. I hide the butchered lamb in my old cavern, so it will not be found with any ease at all. Then I quietly make my way back to the barn.

Avicia comes to find me. "Paen, could you keep an eye on mother? She is going to market today, to try and sell some of her skins, vegetables jugged hare and rabbit. She did not want to trouble you."

"Avicia that will be no problem at all."

"Keep your eyes open, there a lot of vagabonds, vagrants, beggars and guttersnipes about. None of them friendly, only too happy to steal from lonely old ladies."

"OK, her safety is my concern."

As our mother sets off on her journey to the weekly market, I change my guise once again into the wolf. When I was younger, I often used to wonder what this tingling sensation was. Now I know that I am not a young boy. But a young wolf, I look down at the old scar, from where my mother, the she-wolf bit me, so many years ago. I can only assume this is the cause of my transformation. My will to survive over these lonesome days. But now I have a pack to look after.

Like a silent shadow I stalk our mother, keeping her safe, out of harm's way. But the roadside, like Avicia says, is a very dangerous place first thing in the morning. I sense someone else, within a very close vicinity, following very close to the mother of our pack. I drop back, cross to the other side of the driveway. I can smell and see him all at the same time. A youngish man, with a billhook in his hand. Obviously eager to do some damage to someone. Well, he is not going to damage our mother. Stealth, silence is my fortitude in this form. I pounce, clamping my vicious long teeth across his throat, draining his life force in an instant. With no resistance or reticence, I dragged him deeper into the scrub, just past the wood line.

As we approached the village, I kept my distance. But I was circling, avoiding the crowds, so I could always see mother at her stall. Her goods seemed very popular. So when her selling was done, she walked around the market, talking obviously to people she knew, shown by the greetings they give each other. This is my first visit, my attention is drawn to a group of disreputable beggars, trying to muscle in amongst the crowd. I see their hands dipping into the pockets of our mother, snatching her small bag from her arm. Then just as the cowards that they are, they make a run for it, out of the village, across the open road and into the nearby woodland. There were three of them, as I give chase; no one has seen me. Fleet of foot, I am a shadow never seen. Their scent is so fresh it is so easy to follow. They stop to share out their ill-gotten gains, thinking they have gotten away from everyone. But they have not eluded me! Again with the advantage with me, as always. I attack not confounded, sure of the kills. Three dead men surround me. Hidden far from sight, they can languish together forever more, this hapless trio!

I rush to the village, clutching Mother's hard-earned cash and goods close to me. I find her sitting in the shade, recovering from the shock of being attacked, still dazed, I transform back to my human form.

Walking up to her, I pick her up and sit her on a bench that is close by.

"Mother I have your goods, all here."

"Paen, how did you know?"

"Avicia sensed you were in trouble, so I said I would come and see. I am glad I did now."

"I am ready to come home now. Let me walk alone."

"OK Mother, but I will be close by, so do not worry."

"I know, I will feel safer knowing you are close to me."

So I drift back into the roadside, hidden by the woodland, scrub and bush as my fragile mother wends her way home.

I can sense that the droveway[1] is clear for quite a distance. But I still hang back, out of sight, not wishing to be caught at unawares by anyone or anything lurking. Anyone hiding, along this unkempt public highway. We finally make it home in one piece, where I regain my human appearance before confronting mother and Avicia, at the home, where my sister has been doing the cooking. Once mother has put everything away, calmed herself and hugged me, Avicia wants to know how mum is, as well as all the gossip.

"Mum, did you have any problems, out there all alone?"

---

[1] Droveway: Along such tracks a Drover would take his cattle

"Not at first. It was when I had finished selling everything and bought the goods we needed. I was just saying goodbye to a few friends when I was attacked by three men. They stole all that I had. I thought my end had come. But then from nowhere, Paen came. A godsend I say. He even managed to recover my few groats, as well as the goods I bought."

"Paen, how did you know that all this was Mother's belongings?"

"I did not at first. Once I was on the outskirts of the village, I saw three men in a huddle, counting something. They looked like beggars. So I thought whatever they had, did not belong to them. I scared them off, picked up all the stuff, because it belonged to someone else. Then carried on into the village, where I found mum had been accosted. It was then I guessed it was hers."

"I am pleased I sent Paen to meet you, Mum. You can tell me the rest of the news over dinner. Also, while I remember, one of the sheriff's men came knocking, asking if I had seen any strangers about over the past few days. I said no, so Paen, you will have to lay low, just to be safe."

"OK Avicia, I will hide further away, so there is no chance of them finding me. Will that make you both happy?"

They both nod in agreement as we sit together, eating, smiling as the two of them talk as only two women can. Whilst the two of them sit and chat about the day at the village fair and market, I sneak off over to the cathedral's smallholding. There they have some plump chickens, which will help the three of us no end. I take a couple, causing the least amount of fuss. Then cloaking in my lupus form, I run to my old home where I can still sense my wolf-mother. So it does not feel strange at all, being here. The two ladies of the house have shown me how to pluck chickens, how to clean and wash away all the entrails. Once that is all done, I bury all the feathers and contents at the back of my small cavern. I bolt down to the homestead, putting the chickens away in our hidey hole.

Just as I am about to leave, Avicia comes in.

"Where have you been?"

"Just away at my hiding place."

"Can you show me where it is?"

"Why do you want to know? It could put you in danger."

"So that I know where you are, when you are not here. We both want you to be safe, we do not want to lose you."

"OK, but we will have to run. I will bring you back, when it is dark. Just go and tell Mother where I am taking you."

Avicia comes back out, smiling,

"Mum knows that I will be back later."

We race off together, across the Lea and meadow into the surrounding woodland. Up one hill and down the other side; hidden from sight. I take the young lady into my hideaway.

"Well, this is it, all the comfort of home. I hide right at the back, so no one can see me."

"Show me."

"OK, just follow me, stay close."

Taking her all the way back, to where I have made it quite comfortable. There is very little light, but it is out of the cold; the entrance cannot be seen. You cannot hear anything.

"Avicia lay down, see how comfortable you can be."

So she makes herself comfortable as I check the entrance, making sure there is no tell-tale signs of anyone being here. Feeling more like a wolf than a young man, I inspect and find nothing. So I go back inside, in my human form. I find Avicia completely at home.

"Paen, why do you always go around naked?"

"Because I feel comfortable this way. Even before you found me, I was like this, as far as I can remember."

"Come and lay beside me."

I lay beside her, as she strokes my hairy body.

"I cannot believe how hairy you are, Paen. It is as though you are covered in a rug. It feels like silk, how do you look after it so well?"

Then something else takes up her interest. She holds it in her hands, watching it grow. She is really fascinated; the more she rubs, the harder, thicker and longer it gets.

"Lay on your back for me, Paen."

I lay on the wolfskin, my legs splayed for her. She has been naked the whole time she was talking to me. Obviously she had something planned while she talked. Her two orbs, that hung from her chest, she gyrates and rubs hard against me. Her nipples grow thick plump; she puts them in my mouth, I start sucking as though she is feeding me. Avicia closes her eyes, I still feel her hand, rolling back my thick skin, exposing my red, shiny opulent crown. She then climbs above me, slowly lowering herself onto me.

"Paen, I have been wanting to do this for ages, with you. I see you naked very day, your body makes mine tingle. This is my first chance, I do not want to waste it all, by just talking."

"This may not mean much to you, Paen. But I am a virgin. You are my first real taste of man, sex. Of being penetrated. So be gentle."

"OK Avicia."

I lay back, fully exposed, not quite knowing what to do. As she slides down so slowly, I squirm, eagerly thrusting up into her. I feel strangely calm as she cries out! Avicia stops for a second; then elated; she finally takes all of me. She comes to rest on my chest; her lips find mine, rubbing them against my lips, mouth, making me react to her bodily contact. I wrap my arms around her, holding her in place. She gyrates against my hardened meat, making me thicken, pulse, rub my groin against hers.

"Paen, you are so comfortable, I can hear your heart beat. Hold me tight while I sleep here with you deep inside me."

"OK Avicia, but at some time I will have to take you back home."

"Not yet, let me enjoy you; you can enjoy me too. So next time, it will be easier for both of us. Do you enjoy being inside of me?"

"Yes Avicia. Now that you ask, it gives me a thrill, it makes me feel alive. I need you and your body. Now that I have tasted this sex, it makes me want more. Is that the way it should be?"

"Oooh yes, Paen. From what Mother tells me, it gets better the more times you do it."

Wrapped in the wolf, boar and hart skins, we both nod off, Avicia on top, cradled on my chest, her face in mine, our arms keeping each other safe. I awake. Avicia is still asleep above me. I withdraw from her delectable young body. Holding her, laying her back down amongst the furs, I get some meat together, some pelts, the chicken feathers. I put them altogether in a bag. She again puts her arms around my neck. It is still dark outside. I change into my wolf guise, the silver shadow; without a second glance, I bound up the hill, across the same lea, meadow and open farmland. Not stopping until I get safely indoors, I put Avicia into her bed, the bag by the fire. Then I go back out to the barn, hiding myself there, ready for the start of a new day. I am sure Mother is going to the village again today, so I will escort her once again. I did eat, before I left my cave; but I do need more than a single piglet to satisfy my hunger. I am sure that is why the sheriff's men have been around lately, looking for strangers. They have also found the dead bodies of the three beggars and the man at the side of the droveway. So I have to tread very warily, now.

Mother arrives in the barn.

"Paen, thank you for the bag. That will be a real treat, to sell that at the market. Are you going to come with me?"

"Mother, I will be very close by. I do not want to be seen, just in case the sheriff is still lurking and checking on strangers."

"Come and have some ale and a bite to eat, before we go then."

Avicia looked and smiled as I entered the farmstead. I smiled back, trying my best to hide myself as I felt myself stiffen in her presence. She noticed too, and rubbed herself beneath her smock.

"I just need to get the rest of your pelts, Mother. Will you give me a hand Avicia?"

We run over to the barn, where Avicia takes hold of me between her two hands. That feels good, as she rubs slowly. I raise her smock, then, not quite sure what to do I kneel in front of her. I then lick her groin, pushing my tongue between her two love lips. I hear her moan as I push deep, seeing her white juice, I lick at the trial as it runs down her thigh.

I feel hot as I stand up. Avicia looks at me, smiles and eats me. Squeezing me as she sucks, I can feel her tongue prance on top of my expanding muscle. Ejaculate everywhere, I wipe her face, we kiss - having once again enjoyed each other. We rush back to Mother.

She ties her stuff across her shoulder, saying goodbye to Avicia. We went our way once again to the village of Bosco de Warley. Mother on the well-trodden track, used by everyone going the village. Myself, less obtrusive and visible, walking, hiding in amongst the verge scrub and unkempt fields to the side. This time there were no threats, no one hiding on the roadside. So everything was safe with our inward journey and we made good time. Mother was welcomed by everyone with open arms. All pleased to see her safe and well, especially after her last visit when she had been attacked and robbed. She set up her little stall, with all her offerings on display. I kept my distance just like before. I noticed a couple of officious-looking guards with a mastiff between them. So I vanished into the background, not wanting or needing the dog to be able to smell me, catch my scent, or know that I was there at all I was downwind of him, so I resumed my escort duty from a very safe front.

The two of them were in and around the village square, all day long. Not bullying or degrading anyone, which did make a nice change. The dog looked defiant, ugly and large, just like it was meant to be. To be there, to scare off any unwanted vagabonds or vagrants, causing distress amongst the villagers. Yet all went well, again Mother came away, having sold her wares, having made some trades. She smiled a lot, said all her goodbyes, it was a little darker this time so she stayed a little later. Once she was outside the village, I walked a little way with her, to show I was still at her side. I could not smell or sense anyone close by. So we talked, to make the journey home a lot more enjoyable. As we approached the farm it was dark, so I saw Mother to the front door and safely inside. Then I went to the barn, where I planned on doing some work, to make it less exposed to the elements. Repairs were always needed, our hidey-hole needed to be more discreet as well. The hideaway was dug a little deeper, at the back of the barn. The barn was tidied, a few slats repaired. All the tools were sharpened and cleaned, everything ready for a great day's work. Also, the crown and church would be around soon, for their tythe and tax.

The sheriff would be along too, for his tax. So everyone would be paying us a visit, soon for all their collections and dues to the church, as a taxpayer to the king.

Putting down a fresh layer of straw, I lay down thinking of the game I had taken from the king's forest: the boar, the hart. The minor spoils of the rabbit and the hare. But the richest fare had come from the bishop's kitchen and smallholdings: the lamb, chicken and cattle. It had all made our lives easier, to be fed by the parochial, despotic and hallowed church. Of course all unbeknown to him. But I am sure both the King and the bishop will both find out eventually. Then there will be hell to pay.

# CHAPTER FOUR

I have watched Avicia grow up, from a willowy, downtrodden girl to this breathtaking jewel of a maiden. She is now courteous, buxom, her skin the colour of midnight. Her eyes simmering, brown and so big. Her hair is the colour of the crow, her smile so enchanting, it draws you to her. When she talks she entrances, making you loth to miss a word she says. She is a young woman exercising her freedom, wanting to share every moment she has with those closest to her.

When she talks to me. I feel my inner beast calm, subside, wanting no harm or hurt to come to her. I want to protect her from any danger, no matter how near or how far it is from me. Just like our mother, our family is everything. When she holds Mother's hand, along with mine, I feel the circle is complete. My destiny is here with these two women. Should anything happen I need to be here, to react, contain, breech the disaster whenever or whatever is to befall us. I need to be the physical catalyst that saves us from the treachery, the doom that is coming our way. These were the thoughts of Paen, at this time in his life.

William de Bohun, the Earl of Rutland was once again charging his sheriffs with their duties, involving the collection of the King's taxes.

"I want you to take the dogs with you, the greyhounds, mastiffs and the lymers. Because this time, I want to insure that we capture the insurgents, agents, poachers, whoever, that are stealing the game from the royal forests. We are losing both the boar and the deer at an alarming rate, we need to put a stop to it. Is that understood?"

"Yes your lordship, we will take all the dogs with us to ensure complicity, to root all the villains, whether it is just one or a dozen."

"Make sure you do, I do not want any failures or excuses. Especially as we never found out who killed those four beggars, vagrants, just outside Bosco de Warley. Their deaths were horrific, I do not want any repeats of those, is that clear? I want us on the road, by first light in the morning."

"It will be as you ask, we will make everything ready now."

As the sheriffs leave, the earl makes his way to his countess, seeking out her soothing techniques amid this worrying time. She is still laying naked on their bed, where he left her first thing. He flings off his robe and doublet, removes his stockings and, kneeling over Godyth his enlightened wife, kisses her red lips with such eager force. She seeks his groin, making him hard with her two hands, rubbing pulling squeezing his sac, all at the same time. Once he is erect and ready, she rubs his swollen dome against her own moist lips, letting him penetrate her, deep and hard as he pushes forward. Her hands pull his buttocks towards her; his hands are on her divine cheeks pulling her up, onto his proud stiffness.

The serfs are all going about their business, cooking, toiling, cleaning apartments, trying their utmost not to be seen by anyone. The butchers get the livestock ready for killing for the next meal. Choosing the vegetables as well as the fruit for the sweet dishes that are to follow. Life outside goes on unhindered, as it does every day, without interruption. In the bishop's palace all was not well. He was annoyed, angered by the fact that someone or something was stealing from him. He had lost numerous chickens, lambs and calves; something that had never happened before. He could not afford to lose face, he had to find the culprit so he could make an example of him. He had already checked all the staff he had within his boundaries. Nothing was amiss there, so it had to be an outsider. It was not the fact that he would go hungry. He knew in all certainty that he would not. It was just the idea that someone was stealing from the church; the guile, the enterprise was not lost on him. Especially as he was just about to tuck into his five-course breakfast, which had just been freshly cooked before being displayed on his magnificent dining table. He called for his archdeacon, John de Offord. He was found in the vaults pouring over some scriptures. Informed the bishop wanted him, he picked up his tablets ready for scribing. He had his accounts and list of missing livestock with him too. He hurried with all haste over to the bishop's chambers.

"Your excellency, I am here at your disposal."

"Good day John. So tell me, what is actually missing from our pens?"

The bishop carried on eating his breakfast, not offering to share with the archdeacon, or even offering his loyal assistant a seat.

"Your excellency, having gone through all our holdings for the past three years, it would seem we have lost twelve Rhode Rocks, twelve Blue Bells. The lambs, three Clun Forest, three Dalesbred, four Border Cheviot. Finally the calves, two Red Poll, one English Longhorn, two Chilham. This has carried a shortfall in our books of one pound, two shillings, ten pennies. That if I may say so, your excellency, is quite a sizable amount."

"Can I assume we do not know when this has occurred?"

"I can only assume that it has happened during the course of the night. What do you want to do about this problem?"

"I want to find the suspect, culprit. Whether it is man or beast, I want to put a stop to it now. If it is a man or men, I want them caught. If it is an animal, then I want it killed; the body put before me very soon." Archdeacon John de Offord replies.

"I know the Earl William de Bohun is sending out his tax collectors soon. We need to gather in our tithes and rent. So I thought our wagon could join his entourage. See what we could discover together. Perhaps catch the villain unawares."

"That sounds like a good plan. Send one of our riders over to the earl, ask him if we can join his train."

"It shall be done now, your excellency. I will make sure everything else is ready for the collections. So that we are able to go at a moment's notice, if need be."

As the bishop, John Gynwell, takes another gulp of his wine, he waves his deacon from his audience so he can finish his breakfast in peace. The deacon wastes no time at all. He sends one of the church riders directly to the earl of Rutland's castle. He mustered the rest of the draught oxen, their carts and the tax collectors, along with the outriders, needed to protect the tythes and rent when safely collected from their tenants and diocese. So all was in readiness. He then disappeared down to the crypt, down along the cool, damp vaults to his table. He lit his beeswax candle from his tinderbox, so he could see his work surface where he has all manner of scripts, manuscripts, scrolls and parchments laid bare. He put down his jug of mead next to his goblet followed by his plate of cheese and bread. The deacon smiled such an ungodly smile, then poured himself a measure of the mead and took a mouthful. Enjoying its sweetness and warmth he then took a bite from his fresh loaf, along with a piece of the cheese. Then immersed, he buried himself amongst all his papers set before him.

The bishop, fed and relatively happy with himself said a short prayer. Then going back to his bed chamber to console himself after the loss of his livestock. He immersed himself into the delectable body of the cook's daughter. This was so her family could be fed, as well as keeping their home safe within the church's walls. So another young girl was corrupted by the greed, power and hypocrisy of the church.

Regardless of her age, which was seventeen, or being nubile and so nimble, he gets to enjoy her young body above him. Having taken her virginity, broken her maidenhead, he used her for his personal sexual fantasy. Now still touching her large, firm round breasts, he violates her erect nipples with his eager podgy fingers. Telling her to make him hard, her hands cajole his semi-rigid meat. Finally feeling him rise after her ministrations, then thicken, she climbs onto him. Feeding his manhood into her tight little cavern, her warm loins gripping him as she adjusts herself to get him all in. Then she rides him slowly at first, listening to his grunts as he lunges into her forlorn little body. She squeezes her thighs, wanting him to cum. So she could relieve him, leave him satisfied. So she could go and clean herself. Then await his next call, which would probably be after his next meal.

The deacon was aware of the situation. The bishop's liking for young girls. Not necessarily virgins; but if that happened, it was always a bonus, something extra to enjoy. The longevity of the relationship depended on how entertaining the girl was, or could be. This one had lasted some time, due to the fact that the cook's daughter does all the work for him. She relieves him every time, too.

The rider returns, seeking the archdeacon. He makes the trek from the vaults, resurfaces from the crypt. All happy that he has had such a swift reply. The rider is dismounted, awaiting the deacon in his offices.

"So, young Alfred, what did the earl have to say about our proposal?"

"Deacon, he told me tell you if you can get your train ready, for the morning; they will come by and let us join their wagon and guard, just before midday."

"That seems fair. We make sure everything is ready by tonight. I will be inspecting the train first thing in the morning."

Alfred added, "They said they were looking for a poacher, vagrant, or as a last resort a wolf. So they would have their dogs with them. So all being well, we should be able to sort out the interloper in a single swoop."

"Away with you Alfred, I will see you in the morning."

John de Offord, the archdeacon, went up to the bishop's chambers, requesting an audience with him. He is shown in,' waiting at the bishop's pleasure. Bishop Gyngell, having thoroughly taken his pleasure from Malyna, the cook's daughter. The treats of her gentle persuasion, had emptied him completely. He felt spent beyond measure, he was taking a liking to Malyna and her ways!

"Malyna, you stay there, until my return."

He dresses himself appropriately, then goes at a slow amble across his vast chambers to see his deacon.

"John, so good to see you again. What have you got to tell me?"

"The earl will be here about midday tomorrow, with his ox train. So we can attach ourselves to it, therefore benefiting from his guard."

"Anything else of any relevance?"

"Yes, your excellency. They will have their dogs with them. Someone has been helping themselves to the King's boar, as well as the deer. So with their help, we hope to solve this injustice, once and for all."

"Will you be going with them?"

"Yes, so I will be away for sometime, your excellency."

"I will miss you, John. But your presence will be required."

"I have Thomas de Herdwick, in my place, until my return. He will be at your beck and call, should you need anyone."

"I will be saying mass, in the cathedral, this Sunday. So Thomas can see to the congregation, at the chapel here."

"I will inform him, thank you for your time, excellency."

John returns to the vaults, to tidy up, until his return. Also, to inform the sexton, Thomas de Herdwick, of his duties, whilst replacing the deacon. He has a very restful, blameless sleep. His only thought, to return with the vagrants and beggars or the dead body of the wolf, that was stealing the church's livestock.

The bishop, John, returns to his bedchamber; his bed all freshly made, laid down already for his immediate use once again.

"Malyna, so where are you hiding? I will find you my little jewel. I want your sweet, tender body."

"Just here your excellency. Just refreshing myself with a little eau de cologne to keep you interested in me. So what are we going to do with you, now?"

The earl entertains his court for a little longer. Then kissing his lady very firmly on her bright red lips, he takes her by the arm, gently taps her on her rump and smiles as she strokes his rising manhood. They make their way to the big open bed in their private bedchamber to enjoy the promise of the gentle tap, and the pressured stroke on his genitals.

The sheriff's ox trains, dogs and militia were already to set out at first light. They just waited patiently for William de Bohun to take the lead, with the train. It was a slow parade, through open land, eventually to meet up with the archdeacon and his awaiting collectors and outriders. Greetings were short, cryptic and welcoming. The now extended wagon train made its way across the county. Wending in as much of a straight line as it possibly could. Setting up camps just outside the villages, the tax collectors, along with tythe and rent officials, all split up so as to cover as much ground as possible. All the businesses, farms and other dwellings were approached. First the taxes were collected, the dogs being kept on short, tight leashes as searches covered all the forest, the surrounding woodland and hills. Then the church's men made their way through them, claiming its tithes, as well as the rent from its tenant farmers and other home occupiers. The rent that was due to the over-exuberant, wilful church, cripples even the most capable of its tenants. But the church is not concerned about the survival of its beleaguered congregation. It is a suppressor, just as big as the King, when it comes to everyone else's freedom. Just wanting its dues, regardless of the price to everyone else, as long as it can keep its granaries full. As long as they can feed their bishops, archbishops, deacons and all its other hangers on. The Holy Roman Empire, all powerful, belligerent, opulent and greedy. So it was bred from the top all the way down, to the bishops in their palaces, to show no concern for the people as long as they paid their way and paid it to the church. The priests fared just as well as their congregation, they survived on charity most of the time, but not from their bishops, but from the people they served.

Nothing of the wealth from the church filtered down as far as the lowly priest. They were inflicted with poverty because they lived below the salt. They mixed with the common people. No one cared about the priest or the commoner, least of all the bishop of the diocese.

Paen had noticed all the extra wagons included within the train. Also the barking, baying of the dogs being held within the circle of wagons. They were large, vicious, drooling, antagonized by something! They had no friends other than with their own personal handlers.

So during the night he raced back in his transformed state, as a wolf. A short way from the homestead, he changes his guise back to a young man and entering the house, confronted mother and Avicia, telling them both of the wagon train and dogs, obviously making their way here, at some time or other. Telling them that it would be good idea, to empty their hidey-hole. That he would remove it completely, take it away, bury it before it was found and connected to the three of them. We would for the time being have to survive on what we had produced ourselves. Until the King's men and church wardens had done their duties and left the district completely.

So the wagon train had been on the road for some weeks. Finally coming the last village, as well as the surrounding countryside. The last temporal zone. Finally to the area where the killings, murders of the vagrants took place. As well as the theft of the church livestock, the last area of forest and woodland, where the culprits of the poaching of the King's deer and boar were most likely to be found.

Mother's farm was a freeholding, so she would only be expected to pay the tythe to the church. So she had her warrant ready to show, just in case there was going to be any sort of argument.

"Mother, Avicia, are you sure you are both going to be safe? If you are not, I will stay. But I do not want questions asked about me that we cannot answer. I do not want to leave the two of you alone, but I will not be far away."

"Paen, we will both be safe. We have never had any problems in the past. Just make sure everything looks normal, then there will be no problems."

I kiss Mother warmly, hold her close.

"I will be back as soon as they all leave."

Avicia comes very close to me, rubbing her groin hard, roughly against my aroused manhood, squeezing tightly with all five fingers as she kisses me long on my lips. Mother smiles a knowing smile, so having said my goodbyes I leave once again, heading towards the barn to stifle any smell; to destroy, remove any remnants of meat, hides, skins that should not be there. Under the shadow of twilight I mark my territory, just as a wolf would. I loped off into the shadows, to my cavern. I do exactly the same there. Masking my presence as well as my scent. I lay my old hideout bare of everything; the remains of old kills, old meat, bones and skins, anything that give a clue to someone or something having resided here, or spent any time here at all. The evidence was scattered, buried or washed away by the river that was close by. What was visible only had the scent of wolf attached to it. I was left with a couple of venison steaks, which I was just about to discard; but a couple of vagrants passed me by. I quite happily gave the cuts to them. That put a spring in their step as they thanked me, and whistled a tune of some sort, planning on where to cook it.

Now I just lay low, hiding myself way. I came out only once or twice, see how close they were to Mother's and Avicia's farmstead.

They started out actually in the village of Bosco de Warley, collecting the taxes. Putting the dogs out to search for anything that should not be about; the smallest detail not to be missed, in this patrol and investigation. Their dogs did come across the two old vagabonds and some of the old venison. So before they could actually enjoy any of it, they were arrested, clamped in irons and loaded onto one of the wagons, ready for the long journey back to the castle of the earl of Rutland. Having finished in the village, they turned around making their way back to the outlying woodland, forest, scrub and farms. Paen had to show considerable control and patience when they all came to a halt at Mother's freeholding. Mother and Avicia were both ready with their taxes and tythes, ready to hand over willingly to the King's tax collector, as well as the tythe to the church warden. Regardless of this, the barn and house were both searched, by the dogs and the militia. Avicia had opened some of her mead and ale, as well as making some of her vitals available to the King's men and wardens. Avicia and mother bought out some maslin, smoked eel, black pudding and three different varieties of pottage, all of which were all enjoyed immensely. It made their stay far more enjoyable too. First the business of going through the nearby forest, as well as the leas, meadow, woodland and surrounding scrub. Mounting the outlying rocks and crags too, they found some of the old bones and rotting meat. The dogs cowered somewhat when they came cross my scent, but they were pushed forward to rein in the whole area. The cavern was discovered, but was devoid of any material evidence. So they had their two beggars, some bones and the venison found in the beggars' possession. So they would be accused and then summarily dealt with. They all returned to the encampment, happily partaking of the ale and food provided by the two women. William the earl, seemed particularly taken with the beauty, elegance and grace of the young Avicia. She tried her best to ignore him but, the harder she tried, the more playful he got.

Mother whispered in her ear:

"Avicia, do not infuriate him too much, just play a little with him, just to keep him happy until he goes."

"OK Mother, I will just tease him a little so as not to belittle him in front of his men."

William insisted on pawing her as he drinks a little more. Touching her, calling her uncouth names, he makes bawdy statements and ribald comments. Avicia tickles his chin and sits on his lap. She feels just like a trollop. This behaviour is so unbecoming from a man of his station, but she will do anything to keep the peace, so the earl does not lose face or stature amongst his men.

Paen comes a little closer, just in case he needs to alleviate the growing problem. Yet he steals a little too close without checking his position, making the dogs growl, then howl and bark. Then thinking on his feet, he metamorphosed into the silver shadow. Then he raises his head and, baying at the moon, makes himself heard across the whole county, and how far beyond. With this he gives an uneasy feeling to the night. Unsettling everyone, the handlers freeing all the dogs at once, who gave chase. Not sure of what they were chasing, they charged headlong into the forest, to give chase. But they were soon back, with no sign of the offending wild dog, wolf or whatever it was. A few of the dogs were marked, physically with the signs of fighting - but nothing else. After that the camp was settled, fires left lit and guards set to watch the train of oxwains. Silence settled over the homestead once again as all retired for the remainder of the night.

At first light the train was on the move. On its way to the castle, all the dogs in tow, the two vagrants in trammels. All the taxes, rent and tithes collected. Everyone happy to be returning back to a life of normality, for a while at least. They headed into the murky morning light, back the way they came. The earl hoped to get to his castle, the archdeacon to his crypt, within the next couple of days at least. It would be a quicker journey home, as they did not need to stop anywhere on the way; even though the covered wagons were laden down with all the extra weight, of the farmers and villagers hard laboured taxes; heading for the King's treasury eventually. The King and the church, not very highly thought of, both slowly losing respect, due to their complete unconcern, disrespect and mistreatment, an undercurrent of revolt, could be felt if you were close enough to the community.

Paen came from his hiding place. Mother and Avicia both came out to greet him with open arms. They both almost asked together:

"Did you hear that howling last night? It was very unsettling."

Paen took hold of both of them in his strong, muscular, welcoming arms.

"I did hear it, from where I was hiding. It was strong, overpowering. It sounded like a wolf. A large single one. Have you ever had wolves here before?

Avicia replied, with such big open eyes:

"No, this has been the first time, since I can remember."

Mother added, that some time ago, the forest did have some, a lone mother with some cubs. But it had not been heard of for such a long time now. Perhaps she and the cubs had moved on, or even died out there somewhere.

"William de Bohun, the earl, said they would be back at some time, to mount a proper search, within the forest and surrounding woodland for him. He could be the one who is causing the damage within the King's forest, with the death of all his game. As well as the one demolishing the bishop's livestock."

Mother kissed him, pulled herself closer to him, as Avicia added:

"I hope it is not too soon. I did not like the earl, with his offensive remarks. The way he kept touching me, in front of his men. But that is forgotten, now you are back Paen."

Avicia kisses him on his lips, smiling as he holds them both close to him as they walk together back to the farmhouse and sat down around the fire. Reheating the food that was left from the night before, all three of them enjoyed the secluded company and a communal breakfast, shared just like always.

"You two go and get the plough, while I clean up."

"OK Mother," they both chant together, as they take a stroll over to the barn.

Within the confines of the barn, as soon as we are out of sight of Mother, the splendid young maiden kneels in front of me. Brushing the coarse hair that smothers my body, putting my semi-rigid meat into her mouth, squeezing my gonads. Sucking on me heavily. It was not difficult. She is a vivacious, fabulous young woman. I see her every day. Most of the time, I am incapable of not showing what I think of her. I get hard without warning; I play with myself, when I am alone. When we pass one another, she touches me - ooohhh so gently, like a feather. Then I nearly lose all my self-control. Now she stands before me. Having removed her smock, her body glistens, in the poor, shabby light within the barn.

She has her back to me. I lower myself so I can reach her loins from the back, parting her two tight love lips. I taste her dampness already as I load my tongue all the way in. I push it in, all the way in as far as it can penetrate. She tastes of the sweetest meat, her cream the finest wine. All wet, moist, ready almost straight away. I regain my upright stance, I whisper in her delicate ear:

"Are you ready for me, my loving angel?"

"I am always ready for your love, Paen. Only yours for me."

Avicia stands staying as she is. Her pinkness beckons me, partially open, white and sticky as I put the tip of my red, swollen dome against her lush softness. I push slowly as she thrusts her buttocks up in towards me, to accommodate the whole of my manhood. Gently we come together and; as we touch and engage, our licentious bodies couple. I caress her full ample breasts, tweak her plump long nipples; from where I stand, behind her. I am so enamoured with her; Avicia's soft, warm, compelling wriggling body. I do not want to let her go, once we unite like this. I am sure Avicia enjoys delights in all the physical advances too, especially as she is generally the one that starts them all off. I push into her slowly, as she sighs I nibble the back of her neck. Her juice runs freely, I rub it all over my body, spread it across her hot loins. I set her down on the floor. She kneels on all fours, I lunge deep into her capable body, my thickness filling her to capacity.

"That is gorgeous my love, stay there for as long as you can."

She squeezes her greedy thighs together. Not releasing them, or me until she has been completely satisfied. Just as she loosens the tension I growl; ejaculating. My hot jizz smothering her, I lose all control. Now both of us are more than fully satisfied. I withdraw, smothered in my own cum, retaining some of my hardness. She comes to me, taking me in between her nimble hands rubbing, stroking, cajoling me. Pushing the tip of her tongue into the eye of my hardening meat. Then I watch as I see myself into her eager mouth. Sucking, teasing, rubbing my sac, her tongue laps at the very sensitive parts of my organ. Exploding, I finally give way to her ministrations. She drinks me dry.

Avicia smiles, my juice all over her angelic face. We wipe each other down. My gorgeous, rampant beauty gets dressed. I drag out the plough, ready to start turning over the soil, the hard ground, for replanting. Avicia reminds me which field we need to leave fallow for this year.

After escorting the church's train back to Lincoln Cathedral. The Earl of Rutland explains how they thought that the vagrants were initially the culprits for the loss of livestock, as well as the killing of the game in the forest. But after hearing the baying of a what seemed to be an extremely large lone wolf, on the last night they were camped out, directly by the forest. The howling which drowned out the noise of his pack of dogs, there seemed to be something more sinister out there that needs attending to, at Bosco de Warley. So the two vagabonds had been released, gone their own way.

William de Bohun was now returning to his keep to ensure the safety of his taxes and freshen up. Then sally forth once again with a more mobile force, to deal with the wolf, whether it is a pack or just a rogue on his own. The quest would be to put it down, extinguish its very existence and to make the whole countryside that much safer once again. The bishop blessed the Earl and his party, then they continued on their journey back to the Earls fortress.

Bishop Gynwell, after his supper, was still enjoying the favourable attentions of the cook's daughter. She was just about to put her soft young lips around his rising weapon. Just knowing how to arouse him was the trick. Then use him to her own ends, which made this relationship so rewarding. She had been given bigger quarters, making it easier to house her family, instead of living in the squalid conditions her mother was used to. Then John Gynwell thoroughly enjoyed Malyna and all her techniques. She had mastered them so well, she could make the Bishop cum almost at once, without much exertion on her behalf. While she was in his chambers, she could dress in the fine clothes he got for her, obviously to further his enjoyment as well. They fell asleep side by side; the bishop woke first. Leaving the young girl where she was, got dressed, then waited for the archdeacon to appear in his residence, for the morning's audience.

"Deacon good morning, so how was your journey? Well worth the time and supplies that we collected?"

"Bishop, everything will be topped up for another year. Also, it would seem our thief was a wayward wolf. We actually heard him at our last camp. So we need to bolster our defences, until he is captured or put down."

"The Earl William did inform me that he was expecting to go back to Bosco de Warley, in the near future, to seek, find and in all hopes capture or destroy the wolf."

"Your Excellency, I will not keep you from your breakfast and morning prayers. I will sort out the additional defences that we require. Get them put into place."

"John, I will bid you good day."

The Bishop disappears to have his breakfast, this morning for a change, he has his delightful little Malyna joining him at the table. She sits in front of him, naked. Parting her legs, she points to her pinkness, pushing the bishop's head into her groin.

"Now John, you must lick and suck on me. When my juices flow, drink me, suck harder. You will enjoy me so much more, once I am wet."

The Archdeacon gets all the new and additional fences allotted, gets his workers putting them into place to strengthen his already ample stronghold. He take a small lunch, having thanked the sexton for all his hard work in his absence. While he was away, he has neglected all his other work. But that can wait, he returns to the crypt, down in the dank dimly lit vaults to further his studies. Retracing all his old parchments, scrolls and letters, he lights his candles. Looks carefully for all his indicators; there to find his notation. Now to delve even deeper, his quest now to find his second citation, from the works of Vindictus, a necromancer from long ago. To enable him to move forward with his plan.

The Earl of Rutland drank himself into a stupor, thus followed by a very restless sleep. The thought of flushing out that large wolf from the royal forest playing on his mind. He will need the body of the animal to account for the major loss of game in the King's hunting ground. He will need his best archers, his fastest and most favoured dogs. Check on the armour for his horses, then all would be ready for his return to Bosco de Warley.

So, the following morning, all the preparation was ready. His archers, alongside his dog handlers in the wagon, his favoured lymers and alaunts allotted to their cages are being towed on a separate carriage. They make their way as quickly as possible to the forest. Attempting to flush out the wolf, hiding within the confines of the royal forest.

The day's travelling done, at the very late hour, the sun already disappeared, along with its treasured heat. As the chill of the night approaches they set up camp, placing a guard on all four corners of the base. Sleep comes easy, as it is going to be a very early start in the morning. The first meal is a quick affair. The archers equipped at the ease. The dogs released into the leashes of their qualified owners. The force splits in two, both engaging at separate ends of the wooded landscape. There would be no other meal today until the job was finished, until the forest had been completely roused of any wolf or beast, therein. The barks, yelps and howls of the dogs could be heard for miles in all directions. Especially as they approached each other. The excitement roused their base instinct, alerting their pack mentality, their hunting techniques, their drooling, the impatience to kill, to eat, to rest. But today was not the day.

Nothing was in the woods, the forest. Either it had either moved away or died since they last heard that long, even howl when they were here earlier, collecting the King's taxes.

It had been a long, exhausting day. Back at the lager the smell of fresh food was enticing. The cookhouse was all ready to receive them. Serving stuffed chine, with a chunk of maslin, and a selection of vegetables. Ale and mead readily available for the men. The Earl William, taking his favoured red wine. Again they settled in for a night, in the field. The dogs locked away after being fed. Everything else was ready for a nice early start in the breaking of the dawn the following day.

# CHAPTER FIVE

IN NOMINE PATRIS ET FILII ET SPIRITUS SANCTI AMEN. The Holy Roman Empire was overseen by the Devil incarnate himself. He called himself Pope Clement the Sixth. He gained this esteemed position purely by his wealth, power and the dominance of his family. He was a tyrant, bully and mischief-maker - a noxious beast. All his power and position was gained by extortion, fraud, bribes and other treacheries. Riding, ransacking all the capitals of Europe, he claimed all the treasures, valuables and holy items for his church. But how much was going into his own personal treasury? Most of his pillaging was at the expense of the church. In complete disregard for the poverty of others, he killed all in his wake, especially German Jews. Showing bouts of rancour, if he could not get his own way. As he kills, destroys hereditary blood lines, he has an overwhelming desire to leave his mark, as the pontiff.

Edward the Third did not want this pestilent pope invading his kingdom. Tying him down to the thraldom of The Holy Roman Empire. Disrupting his land, with the self-serving needs of the Catholic church. His was a settled territory, multiracial - a hub of ethnic minorities. No need for it to be unsettled. So without a second thought, he said no to a visitation from the marauding, uncaring Pope. Laying claim to the fact that he was dealing with the plague. Did not want, need nor require any diversions, that would lead him away from the needs of his people. No need for Edward to be coerced into a so-called religious campaign to exterminate the Jews, along with other nonbelievers. So much for faith, hope and charity. So much for the freedom of religious beliefs of humanity. Thankfully the King spurned this odium of Jews. So he never had to deal face to face with this over-radicalized papal upstart.

It came from the east with such devastation. Rampaging, having made a mark across Europe. Now determined to wipe out, parts of England. The Black Death had arrived, in all its ungodliness. The unbridled lust of the plague, tormenting the English population, turned them black by virtue of the bacteria, Yersinia Pestis, which was carried by the flea which lived on the back of the now infamous brown rat.

The population disappeared at an alarming rate. One of the disadvantages of trading with far-off places is, that you bring back goods and trades without knowing what was hidden within. The flea intoxicated with rich pickings, in many cases causing a blemish where ever it went. Nearly killing everyone in its wake. Within a year of its arrival.

In Rutland, close to the village of Bosco de Warley, the farmstead has tried to keep the rats, the fleas and bacteria at bay, without much success. Paen had laid traps and planted poison. But as quickly as he quashed the rats and the scallions that followed, he was still overrun by so many more. The human death toll only rises. So far, he has managed to keep his beloved mother and, even sweeter Avicia safe! But he is not sure for how much longer he can manage to do this job by himself. So in desperation, while the three of them are sat round the fire eating, he asks both of them if they can think of anywhere that would be safe, that they could escape to? Where they would feel secure, away from this dreaded disease? Even if it was just for the two of them, while he stayed here alone.

"I think I do know somewhere, with someone who will help us. She knows me, I know her very well, all my life in fact."

"Is it the one you called Nefatia. You mentioned her a long time ago, when I was so much younger. I remember you calling her the Goddess, because she seemed so ageless."

"Yes Avicia. But we would need to load the cart. Then move out completely, for a while."

"Well Mother, first thing in the morning I will get the horse out and load up the cart. Secure everything as much as possible and you and Avicia can ride on the cart. I will be the outrider. Make sure that you are safe. Stay protected from anyone or anything that tries to attack you or, rob you until we get to our new home, wherever it is."

"Paen I will help you, let us all get a good night's sleep."

They bed Mother down together, making sure she is comfortable, has everything she needs beside her bed. Then he escorts Avicia to her bed, kissing long and sweetly those lips so tender. Paen is then off to his usual sleeping quarters to pass a restful night that is long overdue. He is awoken with a gentle motion. Two moist, loving lips roll up and down the complete length of his rigid penis. After her ministrations, he was rampant and raging; the desire like the devil within him, whenever Avicia was close, even more so, when she was touching him.

"Come on Avicia I know you want me. I never say no, because I want you, just as much."

"OK Paen. try this time to cum inside me, just this once, please. I want to feel your full force as you ejaculate, make me tremble, shake!"

"Yes I will keep inside you, so you get all the pleasuring I can give you, my little sweetheart."

"Then we will get ready for our journey."

"Yes my genteel maiden, whatever you say."

All their love was released. They were both aroused, excited, tormented and desiring their release. A torrent, a stream of juice, sweat and fountain of kisses. They both started getting dressed then got ready for their long eventful trip. When all was ready, they both went inside. It looked empty, Mother was ready. Paen picked her up and sat her up in the passenger seat of the awaiting cart. The gorgeous-looking daughter took the reins and sat in the driving seat, looking as though she had done it all before.

"Are you both ready?"

"Yes we are."

They both nodded as if to confirm their statement.

"I will be close enough to both of you. So if anything goes wrong, or seems amiss. I will see. I will be at your side straight away."

The horse and cart pulled out away from the homestead. Taking up the ruts of the old driveway. Paen disappearing onto the left side of the ancient highway, completely melting into the woodland, bush and the various copses. Without any thought or physical strain, the transformation from man to wolf is immediate. The extra fine sensory organs of the wolf working straight away. Knowing who or what was out there at the moment, no threat or danger lurked or lingered. Nothing of intent blocked their way as they journeyed forward. The werewolf kept his distance, so no one was able to see him travelling at a nice steady lope. No strain or pain. His two favourite women remained safe from all this harm. Hopefully this was taking them both further away from the menace of the Black Death.

"Paen, Paen are you there? We are going to stop for some food. Are you going to eat with us?"

I lope to the verge on this dry, windy day and emerge before them as the young man they both know, love and recognize. I was hardly out of breath.

"I am here, forever watchful over you. Just pull into the field where it is flat. There is a stream, some grass too, so the horse can feed as well as quench his thirst."

Avicia guides the horse and cart onto the open lea. There she releases the horse from the cart so he can eat and drink too. Between us we get the pots out to start the cooking. We all sit together, preparing the meal. I had managed to catch a rabbit along the trial, so I skinned and gutted the little animal, cutting the remaining meat up and tossing it in the pot along with the vegetables. Then we sat there watching it while it stewed, bubbled and cooked.

Avicia piped up with a question:

"I have always wanted to ask you Paen, why do you stay looking so young, after all these years? You do not seem to age like the rest of us! Look at Mother, look at me. See how we have changed. He's got older, our hands are calloused. Yet you, you get bigger, stronger, broader, showing no sign of age at all. Where did you come from?"

"Well as far back as I can remember, I was left for dead, I assume by my parents, in a cold, damp uninviting cave. Avicia you remember, I took you there, more than once. There I think I would have perished, starved and died. If I had not been found, cherished, fed and loved by a young she-wolf. It would seem she had just given birth to a litter of pups. She obviously smelt me and found me just outside. So she dragged me in, surrounded me in the warmth of her pups as they fed from her. There I stayed for the night. Then in turn the small pups died one by one. I was the only living thing to survive, so the she-wolf protected me, fed me, fended for me, kept me warm at night. Treated me like one of her own. As time went by I got bigger and went hunting with my mother. Then as my mother got older and weaker, I fended for her, fed her and protected her, kept her warm at night until finally she breathed her last. Then I had to venture out of my cavern, on my own. One night looking for somewhere warm to sleep, I came across your barn, so I used that. I meant to leave before anyone found me. But Mother came in early, found me naked, all curled up in the hay. I have been with you both ever since. So you tell me, what makes me different, Avicia?"

"I do not know, Paen. But I am very glad it was our barn, you came into and, not someone else's." Avicia smiles up at him.

"Paen it was fate, providence, brought you to our homestead, into our lives. We have been perfect for each other; ever since you arrived." Mother smiled looking deep into his rich, sapphire-coloured eyes.

"I cannot think of living without the two of you, here at my side. Let's eat, it smells just about ready."

Avicia turned to Mother, "How much further do we have to go before we get to the house of Nefatia?"

"We should hopefully get there late tomorrow, providing all goes well, as long as we do not come across any hitches."

"Them let us rest here tonight, get a good night's sleep. Then we can carry on, in the morning."

Both women agree, as they start to eat. Paen turns to his mother and Avicia, "I will make our beds in the shack. I will keep watch during the night to make sure we are all safe. Then we can make ready to travel, first thing in the morning."

Kissing them both very affectionately; fingering Avicia's little hot spot as he lingers with her kiss. He closes the door, sitting in front of it, guarding it with his life until both women fall asleep. Then transmuting to the silver shadow, he lurks in the shadows, invisible to anyone, so silent he cannot even hear his own heartbeat. Such shallow breaths, no exertion, no panic, no fear; guile and retribution, his concern. As his saliva runs over his fangs, past my jaw, onto the ground. Woe betide anyone senseless enough to attack either, or just one of my wards. I crack a few skulls, break some necks; but they are just a few dozen, rogue brown rats, silly enough to cross my path during the course of the night. Something to relieve the boredom.

The sun finally decides to rise, casting its light on the dawn of a new day, a new adventure. Paen sits down by the doors just as Avicia opens it.

Avicia goes in to awaken our mother, while he checks the cart is still in good running order. Making sure the horse has drunk, as well as eaten his fill, then attaches him to the cart and brings him over to the shack. Paen reloads all of their belongings. Then finishing off the previous night's meal, he puts his dainty mother back into the passengers' seat of the cart. Avicia takes up the reins once again and gets the horse out onto the track and into the roadway, travelling in the right direction. They are all off once again with their silver shadow hidden away in the depths and sidelines of the scrub and undergrowth. There he can ensure their all-round safety, while the two ladies save their energy; travelling with some rest, with as much comfort as he can provide for both of them, within the confines of the cart. The short-lived heat of the midday sun passes overhead as they approach their journey's end.

"Let me think. I have to remember the right way, the directions. It was such a long time since I was last here."

"Take your time Mother, we have time on our side, there is no rush," her daughter tells her, calming, soothing her with the softness of her velvety voice. Paen smiles, feeling relaxed, sensing the love, devotion and respect Avicia has for her aging mother.

"Yes, that is it. We have to go right into the woods, to the other side. Hers used to be the only house here, behind a rather large gate."

"Paen, did you hear all the directions?"

"Yes Avicia, I am right behind the two of you. I will not get lost, the cart travels too slow for that."

Off they set, following the tracks to the right, through the dapple lit wood, just as the sun was beginning to fade. There before them was a lovely built house.

"If I remember it is called *Riche Mont.* I now have to remember the sign I need to draw, in front of the gate, as well as the entry word, for it to open for us."

She goes down on her knees and draws a strange pictogram, a three-quarter circle, with an arrow-head pointing towards the gate. Inside a pentagram she inscribes the mark of the sisterhood. Whispering the word with her hands open, she shows piety to the sisterhood. Then as she rises to her feet, the gate opens slowly, giving us entry to the abode. As the gate shuts slowly, softly, of its own accord. Paen looks back over his shoulder, amazed that the gate shuts all by itself and that the pictorial pictogram has gone too. He neither sees nor senses, anyone's presence within the stronghold. The horse and cart come to a standstill at the side of the very accomplished building. Paen lifts mother down first from the cart, then ably assistied Avicia down too. It is always a joy to have physical contact with her, so supple and lithe is this graceful young woman. Mother then summons the door to open by whispering the word, "Gratorious."

It opens before us, again with no aid at all. We all enter unannounced, with Mother leading the way. We are taken completely by surprise as the woman known as, or was known as, Nefatia stands before us all powerful, a magnificent lady, commanding. Mother kisses the proffered hand, indicating for us to do the same, to show our respect to the owner of the house we are in. We are in awe as we view our new mistress, who views us with smiling eyes. She is impressive, inspiring, her skin so much darker than the colouring of midnight. Her long, lush flowing locks and waves of hair are blacker than the feathers of a raven. She has long legs, fulsome, breasts are heaving and a truly gorgeous face. Full red simmering lips. Deep rich tantalizing brown eyes. Altogether, she is a very fetching dominant woman, dressed completely in black, defining every curve, swelling in her body. She smiled at Mother, "It is truly my honour, pleasure to see you once again, Mother, after all this time. My dwelling is yours for as long as you need it."

"We thank you for your hospitality. It is our good fortune to have you as our devoted friend."

"So who are these two children you have with you, Mother?"

"Let me introduce my beautiful daughter to you, Avicia. You met her a long time ago, when she was so much younger, nearly a babe-in-arms."

"Avicia, such a charming name, it is a joy to meet you, once again."

"Goddess, it should be me telling you that this introduction is special to us. The privilege is all mine, I know."

"Nefatia this young boy is special. He came into our lives, just when we needed him the most. Changed it all around for us. Worked for us, with us, shared with us. Made us both so much stronger."

"Paen, you honour my humble dwelling. I hope you will all feel safe and wanted here. So why after all this time have you come to seek the protection of my home?"

"May I speak, Goddess Nefatia?"

"Yes Paen, tell me all you can."

"Well, it is to do with the plague. It is taking over the country. We are being overwhelmed by rats. We fear for our health, welfare, our very existence."

"Then all three of you must stay here. We will try and find the source of the problem, to try and make everything safe once more."

"Nefatia, can I ask how you know my name?"

"I have been around for more than a single lifetime. So my memory is long, I remember many things, I sense things, I have a bond with Mother. So if at anytime, you want, need to ask anything, please do."

"Thank you Mistress."

"No Paen, I am not your mistress; I am Nefatia. In time you will learn more about me. You are so much stronger than you portray. All you have to do, is think of me. Then I will be at your side. But, please all of you, make yourselves at home, be comfortable."

Mother sits down to rest, talking, confiding with the goddess. The two youngsters go outside to unload the cart. Putting their little bits of belongings, in the rooms provided for them. They all had their own room, it was exceptional. Paen goes to put the cart out of sight. He releases the horse into the meadow, where his soul interest is the sweet, green succulent grass. Paen fills the trough with fresh clear water. He then goes into the stable to lay the bedding out for the horse, to save him time later. Avicia catches him just as he finishes.

They go back into the presence of Mother and Nefatia. Sitting down to their first meal together, in such pleasant surroundings. They all disappear to the privacy of their own rooms; it has been a long trek, over the past couple of days. Sleep came easy to everyone, fatigue having taken them over, plus the luxury of a full stomach. They all settled into their comfortable cots. Not a sound was to be heard.

Nefatia appeared in Paen's room, enamored with his strong, vibrant life force, the strength of his will. His character shone forth. His radiance enveloped her, making her feel more than safe. She hoped he was here to stay for quite a while. She bent down to smell him; a strange scent exudes from him. But she will discover what it is why she is so drawn to him. Before she leaves, she gets very close to him, close enough to detach some of Paen's body hair, so she can check what he really is!

She of the sisterhood was alone in her study. Matches the long coarse hairs, against others she has managed to collect, over the years. It looks, feels and smells very familiar. There is only one way to be sure, to verify her conclusions, to complete her investigation. Patience would be the key to understanding him, totally. She willed herself back to sleep, her thoughts of a fine young man rolling around in her memory. This was the first for a long time, but she had never taken the time to be pleasured by a man, of knowing a man intimately. Still a virgin goddess. But all this was a distraction. Was it just a man? Or something more, invading her immediate, sensitive thoughts, this early in the morning?

Paen just had an indirect, fleeting glimpse of the goddess flashing past his very receptive optic nerve. She was the type of lady he had never seen before. Just as he was thinking of Nefatia, she appeared in his room, right at the very moment he thought of her.

"Paen, you wanted to see me? Ask me something? Share something, that you hide from Mother and Avicia?"

"Yes, I would like to know what type of woman you are. I know you are strong and fearless. But you have lived for so long too, I would like to know more about that."

"If I share my life with you, then will you share yours with me?"

"Of course, I will tell you what I remember. If you have any questions, then I will try to answer them."

"In that case, I need to go back to Queen Neferata of the Lahmian court, in Nehekhara, the land of the Tomb Kings of Khemri. She was the first warrior queen. Younger than her cousin Queen Khalida. She was strong, unyielding, feared by all her enemies. She was chasing the elusive 'Elixir of Life'. She captured, enslaved and tortured a dark elfin sorceress to the point of death, before it would reveal the whereabouts of the Elixir. Once she knew where to find it, that was her mission in life. To hold at least a single drop to her lips for eternal life. She teetered on the edge of desperation, carnage and death more than once. Finally discovered the potion, in the Roaming Sands of Kalipha el Mia. Having found it, having gained the longevity, her heart desired. Now she knew where the Elixir was, she was the only person that could gain access, anytime she wished. This is the time she started the sisterhood. Queen Neferata now had supreme control of the valuable elixir. Also knowing that the elfin sorceress could not return to her own kind. Making a wise decision rather than terminating the life of the elf, offered her the position of the Queens swordsmith. The first weapon to be bound to her for Neferata's eternity, however long that may be.

The sorceress left to her own resources, conjured up her own forge and smithy. Hidden away from the Lahmian Court, so she could perform her magic undisturbed. Then she came before Queen Nefatia informing her the sword was almost ready. All she needed was five drops of the royal blood now it was combined with the elixir. The Elfin swordsmith asked my mother which hand she fought with. The right hand was her reply, then she offered in the direction of the enchantress five digits and made the daintiest incision on each fingertip. Each globule collected in its own phial, promising the queen that her personal weapon, would be with her the very next day.

In the forge, the sword was in a pristine state. Releasing the locket at the hilt of the falchion, she released each droplet of blood into the caplets, in the shape of a quincunx. She sealed the locket and with a thought she melded the blood with the weapon. Now the falchion has a scarlet hue as it flashes in the sunlight. Both edges sharp and a bloodstone set in the handle. The sorceress casts it within its velvet box so she can handle it without disrupting it ownership and, song of allegiance to its life-long partner.

The Queen sat on her throne as the sangome enters. The sangome puts the velvet box on its stand and then starts bowing to the Queen, informing Her Highness Neferata, the weapon is now hers. The Queen resplendent rises to take her new sword. Handling it for the first time, she stands agog as the sword flashes a deep red. Resonates sings to her;

*"I am of the blood of the High Queen Neferata. I am sedulous* [2]*hers alone, bound by her blood to protect her for infinity. To strengthen her army. To strengthen her stature within the sisterhood."*

She has a sluggard brought before her. Standing before him the sorceress nods as the Queen smiles. Without any thought of the consequences she takes Sedulous, carving through the body in front of her. Dropping to her knees, Neferata gorges on the heart of the carcass slain before her. Embedded with all is thoughts, memories, his blood and his lowly existence.

The High Queen stands upright, her eyes crimson and bellowing as loud as she could. A powerful strength not seen in her before this very moment. Her long black hair was a burning flame of red. Sedulous aflame with the same intense colour as the elixir seethed within both of them. As she absorbs the new life-force accepting it as her own. Then as Queen of the Lahmian sisterhood glows, the elfin magus informs her that this will happen every time she takes a life. It is the elixir working, bringing the two energies and life-forces together to be as one. Queen Neferata mounts her throne with her legs astride and sedulous thrust high in the air. She then spoke to her sisters, "Men will no longer intimidate us and make us slaves. Nor will they be our tyrants or overlords. They, men, no matter what class or breeding they will be subservient to the Sisterhood of Lahmia. Their lives will be worthless once taken by any of the sisters.

---

[2] Sedulous is the name of the Queen's sword

The response was a tumultuous cheer, falchions raised all with a bright red hue. Then led by the Queen and her enchantress they all retired to the banqueting hall. She has won the battle.

I am living proof her foray assault against an invading force of Templars, who were trying to claim the fortress of the Lahmian Sisterhood for their own depraved satanic purposes. However, they could not withstand the ferocity, kinship solidarity of the sisterhood. Also the fact that the Templars just could not subdue or annihilate the femme fatales. Eventually the Templars were quashed, extinguished and demoralised by their own inadequacy. Finally fleeing this pestilence, they could not control.

The Queen of the Sisterhood exercised one last duty from the youngest of the Templars. On the battlefield in front of her legion of sisters, she disrobed him herself. Making himself ready and then laying him down in the sand mounting him then forcing the knight to copulate into her very warm receptive loins. Working him until she felt his seed inseminate her. Knowing he would give her the daughter she had long desired, having consulted with her Elfin enchantress. She then stood up and pointed to her nearest sister telling her "He is now yours to enjoy Rateema. In which ever way you see fit."

Her falchion Corbie sang as it struck the Templar. Fateema was now down in a squatting position devouring his heart. Her whole body convulsing as she stood upright. As she consumed his life force aflame her whole body lit by the elxir of life.

As time allowed, the sangoma checked on the High Queen's progress, both she and the child were in excellent health. Finally, the time of the travails arrived and the birth had no complications. Then wrapping the daughter in fresh swaddling and laying her in her mother's arms, her first daughter.

Queen Neferata, my mother baptized me, with a single drop, of the 'Elixir of Life'. The sangoma taking me into her powerful arms, gazing deep into my brown eyes, willing and charming me I am sure. I offered my dainty right hand to her there and then. As with my mother, she took a miniscule globule of my virgin blood from the tip of each tiny digit. Casting them away in their own separate phials. Once again the magus disappearing into her forge for days to cast her enchantments onto my own personal falchion. Once it has been forged and then impregnated with the quincunx and then it will be confirmed with my own royal blood. Once I was big enough to hold my personal sword, I had the same ceremony as my mother with only me touching my falchion. It had been finely tempered with my blood and set with two enormous bloodstones in its handle. Then as the sorceress gifted me my falchion. I took hold of it for the very first time and it sang to me in front of all my sisters, "*Princess Nefatia the invincible, my princess. I am your protector, heartbreaker. Never let me leave your side.*" Since that coronation with my falchion, we have never been separated. She has taught me not to bow to any man. I may seduce him, make love to him, help him copulate, entice him with my body - but in the end I will defy him, end his life if I need to; but all for the ends of the growth and domination of the Sisterhood. I originally arrived here a lifetime ago, Probably more than a single lifetime on an Egyptian trader. I have been here for as long as I can remember. I am a virgin vampire of the sisterhood. I have always been able to get my own way, simply by asking. That is why everything seems so completely different over here, to what I had been used to. I am hiding in plain sight. Unless you know where to look for me, you will never find me, no matter how hard you try. My mother relies on me to extend the sisterhood. With such a small populace, it is not an easy task. But I have all the time I need. When I was born, my mother, Queen Neferata, took me into every battle with her. I was attached to her back. When I was old enough, I was given my own horse, I then rode with my mother wherever she went; I had my own sword forged for me. When I was able to lift it, wield it, replace it, into its scabbard, it went with me, it was my guardian. its name is 'Heartbreaker'. I have been using the name Melvina, it seems a lot more welcoming; easier to pronounce."

"But I much prefer, Nefatia. It seems to fit you perfectly. The absolute femme fatale female. I assume it runs in your family. Perfection, beauty, flawless, immaculate."

"It does Paen. I have been waiting for a man to match me for so long, I had all but given up. But now I think I have finally found him. If I have, then I would want him to stay with me."

"Who do you think this man is, this one you have been searching for?"

"You of course Paen. I was studying you last night, as you slept. I took some of your body hairs. I have a feeling there is something you are keeping a secret from Mother and Avicia."

"There is. But let me tell you my story to see if it makes any sense to you. Especially with your worldly knowledge on such matters."

"OK, I will try to help you, as you tell your story."

"As far back as I can remember, my life started for me, by being left alone, on the floor, in a cold, damp cave hidden away in amongst the hills and woodland of Rutland. I never knew my parents, obviously they never did want to know me. But by luck, a young she-wolf was using the same hide-away for her new litter of pups. On seeing me, she dragged me over with her teeth, puncturing my skin. I bled a little, but she licked my wound until the bleeding stopped. Then she put me into the comfort and warmth of her litter. It was bliss for that night. She fed me, nurtured me as if I was one of her own. But slowly her litter of three died, within weeks of giving birth. So eventually she only had me left. She fought for me, fed me, kept me warm, went hunting for me."

Nefatia interrupted, "I think you may have had your problems all along Paen. I would suggest that the she-wolf, when she bit you, enhanced you there and then. Then she just added to your powers when she licked your wound, to stem the bleeding."

"Then when I was old enough, she took me hunting with her. We would tackle kills together. I enjoyed the hunt, the kill, the smell of air, the blood, the silence after the kill. Then the taste of the warm meat, once we were able to rip away the fur, skin and get to the flesh of the corpse. Having my muzzle and my mother's so close to me. That was all the joy I needed then. Then sometimes she would let me go alone. Then I would ride my kill. Find a young deer, run alongside it and jump onto its back. Then clamp my hands over its yielding mouth and nose. I would ride until it fell, snuffing out its life, then bring it back to the den, where we would share the meal, as always."

"Paen, this is definitely where you got your powers from. All that time spent in the company of a wolf. Like I say, the wounding gave you the lupus albus virus, changing you into what you are now, a werewolf. Nothing will change that, you just have to make the most of it."

"It is a rather dark secret."

"Yes, but if I know Mother, she already knows, and I am sure, if Avicia is her daughter, then she will have an inkling too. So it will not be as dark, as complex as you think."

"OK, so the next thing to do is tell both of them."

"Yes, Paen I think it is.

"But first I think we need to check on the other two women we have here in this house. Get a little something to eat as well."

Yet without warning, a cry came from deep within the dwelling. It is Avicia's voice shouting aloud, "Paen, Nefatia, it is mother! I think Mother is dying."

"We are coming now Avicia."

"You must hurry if you both want to say your goodbyes to her."

There she lay on her back, so she could see everyone. As she smiled, her big bright eyes seemed to be so full of life still. The three of us sat around, listening to her every last word.

"Nefatia, you were my first ward, you were creative and a real pleasure to guide. Look at you now, independent, blossomed into a raging, bright flower, ready to handle the rest of your life.

"Mother you are eternal, always in my heart and mind," Nefatia tells her.

"Avicia, my one and only daughter. Your father died so long ago, but loved you, for the short time that he knew you. I loved and adored you for my whole life. You were a special part of me. I felt your pain when he passed away from your tiny life. We have carried each other for all these years. We were one, so it saddens me now that I have to pass on, leaving you all alone."

"Mother I have wanted you all these years. We were closer than one. It fills me with doubt, if I can carry on without you. Now that you are not with me at my side."

"My most loving daughter, I will not leave your side. I will be with you now and forever more, believe me."

"I will always treasure your knowledge and wisdom, dearest Mother."

"Paen, the young boy, who came into our lives just when we needed you most. Just when we needed a man around us. Wild, untamed, defiant, unkempt. But a son of every mother's dream. I know when I go, Avicia will not be alone in this world. In fact I know, the two of you know each other very well, already. Also, the secret you tried to hide from me. I know you better than yourself. Very soon you will disclose that too, to my daughter. Do not be afraid when the time comes."

"Mother you were perfect for me. Not once did you fail to understand me. You guided, trained and mothered me, just like the she-wolf. I have always loved you, I will miss you, but you will always be with me, here." as Paen strikes his chest, showing, intimating to Mother where he will keep her long after she has passed on.

Avicia sat there cradling her mother in her arms, humming a lullaby that her mother taught her when she was still in her cradle. Nafatia and Paen comfort her. All three help her mother, making sure she knows that she is not alone in her moment of passing. The death rattle was short, uncomplicated. Revered by all three, the elder lady passes into her afterlife.

Now Mother had passed on, Avicia, Paen and Nefatia were all silent with their own private personal memories of this kind revered and mystical woman. Paen carries away her still body and, with Avicia at his side; they both follow Nefatia to her personal crypt. Here she is laid to rest within the walls of the Sisterhood. Nefatia singing the battle song of the dead, sending her mother all victorious to her Valhallah.

*"She won her glorious battle,*
*She has always been a victor.*
*Rosina affected so many lives;*
*Cast not her spirit away from you.*

*Take her spirit to your very bosom,*
*Welcome her.*
*Sing her name out loud,*
*So her children can be proud.*
*Rosina, Rosina, Rosina."*

"Perfect Nefatia, your song does fill me with pride. Thank you so much for your praise, allowing my mother to buried here."

"Avicia, Paen, would you like some food?"

They both followed the goddess to where a table was laid with food. As they enjoyed the food before them, along with the fragrant wine, they reminisced, talking about their own times with Rosina, what made her special to each and every one of them. The three adults grew closer and more familiar with one other.

# CHAPTER SIX

The Earl had risen once again, to make an early start on the clearance campaign to clear all the corrupted human flesh, tainted by the black death. Each and every body looked and smelled exactly the same. Black, rotting, blistered, pitted with sores, lethal with any sort of contact. So a pit was sunk, well away from any settlement. The job was going to be a long one. The villagers aiding William in his hunt for the dead, dying, the semi-decomposed; whether young, old, or child! All have to be recovered, disposed of, one way or another. With this as the Earl's main charge and responsibility. He was going to take with him his best swiftest dogs to once again check the forests of Bosley de Warley, to see if he could recover, capture the wolves that devoured the game that went missing, some time ago. His previous visits had found nothing. If it was not wolves, then he did not have any idea as to what ravaged his herds of hart and wild boar. He had to pay dearly to his liege lord, Edward, from his own private purse, to compensate him for the loss. This had left a very bitter taste in his mouth and preyed on his conscience, for a while. So he wanted to settle the score. Revenge would be sweet, satisfying; to turn that rogue wolf, or pack, into a wall or floor covering; just for his own peace of mind. Perhaps even have his chef braise it in red wine. So he could finish it with the final insult; to eat the dog, that cost him so dear.

But time to collect the bodies from this blessed plague and try to contain it and stop it spreading. Throwing the rotting, heaving pile of carcasses into the lime-covered trenches to conceal the dead. Also to stop the spread of this malignant disease.

"Roll out! Come on, let's get this disaster contained. Get shot of these contaminated bodies. We will do it field by field."

Then in turn the corrupted villages will be turned, once cleansed, into the havens they once were. William once again gave, barked his orders, "Here we go forward. Charge everyone to bring out their dead or dying. Then the scourge will be ours to cleanse, to keep England clean and free."

The bishop was also out in force, with an army of priests. Levied to bless the dead en masse, or at any single funeral pyres. To give their souls the rest, peace and forgiveness they required, for their supposed eternal life.

The priests gave support, prayer; readily giving their advice to all and sundry. To those who wanted their assistance. Verbally, or, in the form of vitals, watered grog, small amounts of church wine. All were welcome to imbibe. Alone or together, all the priests were just as poor as their congregation. But they are only too happy to share what little they have with their beleaguered followers. Even more so, if the bishop obliges, by putting something extra out there.

So he keeps the lamb of God visible, still fresh in the heart of their belief. At the same time encourages the strays, non-believers back to a church that cares. Never one to pass up an opportunity, or good chance to preach or talk to his diocese, the good bishop travels on his favourite horse, distributing his bread, cheese, cured meats and smoked eels along with his varied liquid refreshment. All in the hope of extending his favour, authority, across his whole influential area. Many recognise him quite openly, along with his many parish priests he has at his side. The people seem joyous to see the minor pontiff, along with his aides, in the field providing succour and relief to all those that need it. The King failed to contain the death and stench of the marauding bubonic plague. Edward the third, was after his physicians stemming the flow; but as yet nothing had been able to stop or decrease its impact, or the death rate that followed it. His top medical practitioners were unable to come up with a cure, or a reason why it was happening.

John de Offord is alone. Referring to his scriptures, he is lost in his own little world, alone and confident of his letters and notations! The records found amongst all his searches have satisfied him. He has a wry little smile to himself. He found exactly what he wanted from some encrypted letters from an ancient collector called Vindictuss, who dabbled in all sorts of old forgotten beliefs. He practised all and some forgotten various types of dark arts. But all to no avail. He tried, persevered, practised his whole life, but never was truly successful. He was never totally committed. Never immersed deep enough, to turn his soul black, turn his soul to stone. Never enough to shed blood, for his practises. Never greedy enough, to fill his personal desire, to corrupt his very being, with all the earthly pleasures, he could want, gain, with his arts. To exact a lifetime of easy living, at the expense of all else.

Archdeacon de Offord wanted to be completely different. He had already known of the Bishop's liking for young girls. He had never said anything about it. He was sure that the Bishop fancies, as far as the Bishop knew, were a secret only to himself. Also sure his own Bishop was not the only one committing perifdy. He was confident his bishop, if left alone would become iniquitous. John Gynwel, was sybarie and it was becoming uncontrollable. As he had already worked his way through four; made them pregnant. Then with his wealth, sent them to a convent, with a big enough offering to look after them. As well as help with the children's education, when it was required. Obduracy was the way the John de Offord was inclined. He wanted nothing to get in the way, no obstructions or distractions; perhaps all that would come later. Perhaps he himself would enjoy the distractions that at a later date would lighten his life and open his eyes to what the world had to offer, to a worldly man. Once he had conquered all his goals!

He had seen too much mendacity and dissimulation in all the time he had spent with the church. He just wanted a little piece of it, just to see what he had been missing out on. The church itself was recalcitrant. But broken down into its local, component parts, it has all the makings of being inanities. A soulless place. Lost due to its lacklustre leadership. The flock being led astray, not so much by the farmer but more by the shepherds under his direction. Stentorian, a lone voice echoes, rebounds, finally dies in a hall that is meant to be full of people. But finds itself as empty as a winter barn. A voice sounds so forlorn when it commits words to the ether. Then there is no one there to listen to a single word. But who cares, when life is good, whether there is a congregation or not!?

But if you lead the good life, you do not have to work for it. You have the protection of the church, its power and glory, reign over you. When you do not have to labour, just be in the right place at the right time. To receive your daily bread, I just need to be a bishop! So the Archdeacon feels that his exertions, his research, are amounting to an easy life, with its own reward in the afterlife, but also in his real life now. So his present work would take him away, forward and past all his dreams.

King Edward was not concerned about the deaths of his subjects. First he wanted to extirpate the suspects who were trying to overthrow him. He would not rest until all his counterparts were checked then, considered when innocent, were buried in an unknown grave.

The Earl was quite exhausted after the continuing fight against the rats and fleas and the endless flow of dead, violated bodies. There was a smell of burnt human flesh. The site of corrupt, black lifeless forms endlessly burning, burying in mass pits. The heat of the sun, helping with the decomposition, makes the smell stronger, the flies more virulent as they settled on the scabrous, rotting flesh. The whole scene was one of utter despair for everyone. Nauseous, infectious, over run with not only the black death, but typhoid and famine as well. Death was everywhere, unstoppable, malignant, foreboding. The Earl wished he was back at his court with Godyth; perhaps doing the coranto, or even the cotillion. Instead, he was here, trying to stem the irremediable, incurable bubonic plague. At this moment in time he not only felt, he knew he was on the losing side; just like everyone else who was working along side him in the field. Lining the graves with clay, in the hope this might stop the infuriating disease.

The King's doctors and physicians, were all looking for a way to extirpate the rats. Life on the whole was going to be very dire, for some time to come. The King himself was down at Portsmouth with his wife, Philippa of Hainault. Both were seeing off Joan, their beloved daughter with a retinue of four ships. She was off to her betrothed, Peter of Castile. So, in this not such glorious summer, Joan, the most protected woman of Europe, was away to Bordeaux, her first stop in her treacherous journey.

Joan was received in Bordeaux by the mayor, who tried to tell her of the savagery of the Black Death here in Europe too. But ignoring his pleas they stayed in the hope of furthering their journey onwards. But they got no further. Joan died here in Bordeaux, without ever seeing Peter.

The archdeacon was an apostasy, still mulling over all his arcane scrolls, manuscripts, yet at last all coming finally, to fruition. Slowly the light dawns. Again he smiles, such a knowing, ungodly sneer!

Avicia was born with her mother's gift; A siblys and seer. Such a sensitive package, which she thinks she has had, for a lot longer, than she can remember. But since her mother passed away it seems to have caught up with her; often takes her over. At these times she spends alone. But much prefers the time spent with her other two friends, lovers. She knows Paen and Nefatia are going to form an incredibly strong bond together; which has already started, unbeknown to them. She is not entirely sure which of her gifts is the more pronounced. Being an augur seems to come more easily, perhaps because she enjoys it so much. But being the seer at present, comes and goes. She is fascinated by both. Avicia is all bonhomie, so easy-going when she needs comforting, or needs to talk to someone; she knows that she only has to think of Paen. Then he comes to her; no matter what he is doing, he drops it all to come to her.

He still relishes her sweet tight body. He loves to arouse her with his fingers, his tongue and his mouth. She loves it when he is sucking her over-large nipples, they are so sensitive. The soft caress of his lips on her long neck makes the hair stand on end. He puts his tongue in her ear as he twirls her outrageous nipples between his finger and thumb. He can feel her hands on his hardening shaft. He loves to feel her soft, sensitive fingers on him, anywhere she pleases. She knows how to handle his manhood, she has been doing it all her life. He loves to watch her nipples extend and he can feel them plump up between his very eager digits. Avicia loves to be on top as he is pulling on his rigid, rampaging pole.

"Paen, lay down for me, I cannot wait any longer!"

She mounts him, right down to his hilt. As she hits home, she writhes, is dripping wet. Paen is adamantine, Avicia can't help but move uncontrollably. Wriggling and gyrating as his hardness welled up, so full of love. As she pumps him he grunts and he pushes up, exceeding his expectations and filling his first love with his sticky, thick unstoppable juices. Yet again both are satisfied. Smiling, they fall into a mutual hug. Avicia is happy once again. Her visions coming, extolling both their virtues. But the dreams not always as good as the real thing! Talking, sharing with Paen is always a joy, her time never wasted, with or on him. She has kept her beauty, both physical and mental. The external aura has never been dulled, Paen has always seen past it, and fed off her external and internal beauty. Avicia has always been part of him, always will be. Her time spent with Nefatia has been good. She has been very resourceful, she is well equipped, always happy, attentive. To talk is one of her joys, especially woman to woman. It has been one of the things she has missed, over the last few years. So female company, they both really enjoy.

# CHAPTER SEVEN

They feel so comfortable in each other's company. Their shared words, enlightening both their worlds. Nefatia takes Avicia by the hand; she follows coyly, gladly, both smiling, looking deep into each other's eyes. They stop in Nefatia's bathing room. The step-in bath flows with warm white milk, thick, luxurious. The goddess removes Avicia's old, over-worn smock. Avicia tentatively disrobes the alluring, glorious goddess. Together they both walk into the rose-petal liquid. Sitting down beside each other, they softly rub the milk into each other's firm, curvaceous bodies. Both linger with their touch, their soft caresses and featherlike touches. Both are amused by their sense of freedom, fascinated by their arousal and pure unadulterated pleasure and the tenderness they willingly give each other. The goddess made the first positive move. She moved her head, opened her moist mouth and took one of Avicia's excited large nipples, within. Then just started to suck at first. She pushes the tip of her tongue hard against the irrepressible, surging plumpness and lets it wash over her eager tongue. Then she winds her oral muscle around the uneven surface of Avicia's aureoles too. Taking Avicia's hand she places it between her legs and rubbing her hand against her hairy pubis, "Avicia, my sweetness, rub here for me. Softly, gently. I know you have the touch. Good, that is right where I want you to touch me. It feels so good. I love your thick, juicy nipples my love, so tender."

"I am enjoying all your attentions, Nefatia. I love having my nipples sucked. Paen chews a little too, then twirls them between his fingers. But you know my secret places, I am sure."

"Paen has touched your intimate places as well?"

"Yes, he is very good, he has satisfied me so many times. Perhaps you should let him touch you at some time? It would be good for you, goddess. But in your own time of course."

While they were talking, Avicia had worked her finger deep into her tight snatch, toying with her, making her wriggle, making her sticky, licking her own finger. Then she tried two fingers, to excite her even more. Avicia climbed up, then over onto the Nefatia's lap. Taking her face in her hands she kisses her full on the lips while slowly caressing her ear and lobes. The goddess reciprocated, kisses flowing from both pairs of lips. She now fingered Avicia, giving her long deep rubs, making her wet, the bathing all but forgotten. Fingers, hands, fingering caressing, stroking, massaging. Groins, loins interlocked, splashing in the bath. As the two bodies were taunted, pillaged and excited this became a bath time to be remembered, definitely to be repeated more than once. At last the two bodies lay naked at the side of the bath, the smaller body of Avicia above the superb, splayed body of Nefatia, both engrossed in the other. Both were still supple, exposing each other's delights in the often-favoured sixty-nine position. The sweet hypnotic smell of the rose petals filled the air, tinged with the eager licking, sucking sounds of flesh on flesh.

Both women wowed each other. This was the first time for Avicia, to be sexually involved with another woman. But she enjoyed the satisfaction, of every physical touch and caress. She was smitten with Nefatia, so they moved together, as they spend more time, in the creamy cooling bath.

"This is the first time I have ever partaken in such a gorgeous bath, with such a regal, overpowering woman."

"I have enjoyed you too, Avicia. Believe me when I tell you that you are special. That you really are special, such a beauty, with such a soft, beguiling touch.

Out in the open, Paen spends time on the small farm, within the boundaries of the Goddess's abode. He cultivates the vegetables, tends to the wild herbs; loving all the vibrant colours. A few wildflowers have taken hold, which he allows to grow freely as long as they do not encroach upon, nor invade his crops of herbs and vegetables. He also ventures beyond the confines of the *Riche Mont* walls. He needed meat, late at night he has been venturing forth, seeing what spoils he could kill without disturbing the livestock of the royal forests. Already he has found plenty of small game, hares, rabbits and the odd polecat. There has been the odd carcass or two, which has taken the time to clean and, return with. All these have been added to Nefatia's larder, to be consumed as and when the desire for raw meat overwhelms him.

Finally, the lather-rich bath cools and allows the two perfect, lush, supple women to leave. Climbing out hand in hand, their eyes alight, they stop to kiss gently. As they stop, they cannot help themselves - they graze those firm, fabulous breasts, all four of them. They pulling and tweak each other's plump, excited nipples.

"I am addicted to your divine, magnificent body, my goddess. I hope you do not mind me telling you this? It tastes so sweet and tender. Your juices are so thick and creamy, your skin is so soft, vibrant and so touchable. I cannot wait to do this again."

"I am looking forward to spending so much more time with you, Avicia, you are splendid, touching me in all the right places, that is amazing for your first time. While you are here, come with me, use my wardrobe. I know you will find something in here to go with your glowing, brown eyes."

Both women walk into Nefatia's boudoir, adorned with all sorts of clothes - brightly coloured kaftans, silk dresses, silky peignoirs, skirts made from Egyptian linen, so many colours to behold. Avicia takes a liking to an all-in-one pale pink dress, the likes of which she had never set her eyes upon, or seen before. She felt a new woman, bequeathed to her by her fabulous new friend, mentor and ally.

Paen strolls in after a full day at the farm. Sweaty and dirty, he heads for the cooling waters of the well. So fresh, these revive him immediately as he pulls up the bucket, splashing the water over his body. Drying himself with some old cloth, he enters the new home. He is just beginning to get used to it as well as enjoying it due to the quiet, privacy and the fresh air it grants him. His freedom to hunt when he wishes, also to protect and safeguard. All this at his own personal disposal. Now it is time to eat. On entering the scullery, where the two women are cooking, his breath taken away! There before him stood two goddesses of the highest magnitude. Never had he seen women so resplendent, definitely not his beloved Avicia. So regal, dominant, both Avicia and Nefatia's presence and radiance needed to be acknowledged. Inspired, a sign of approval of their magnificence, from such a lowly man, might not be enough; but it would have to be, because he could not offer them anything else.

"Breathtaking, alluring, sensational. Two young women, as glorious as if you came from another world, another time, from my dreams maybe! You both smell fabulous too."

"Why thank you, young man. We were both hoping that you would notice us. We are very glad you did. Are you ready to eat?"

"Yes, I cannot get over the two of you, so majestic. Avicia you in that colour! It shows your eyes like never before."

"Paen, you always notice the smallest things, you are exceptional too."

The goddess smiles, looking directly at him when she tells him, "Paen, the next time we bathe, we will all bathe together. That will be something to look forward to, I am sure. Is that all right with you?"

"I am sure it will be my honour, pleasure and pure delight, joining you two queens in the joys of bathing. It will be enchanting, sublime being exposed to the artistry of your hands and fingers. I am sure it will be unforgettable"

Avicia laughs out loud at her two friends, "In that case let us eat while we dwell on us bathing together. Especially as it has been a long day, for our young man here."

"Tonight I will be checking our perimeters. Those rats excel at being a nuisance. I want to go check, in the morning too."

Outside it is a wretched, people-starved place. The countryside has never been so devoid of human beings.

The following morning Avicia and Paen hitch up the horse with the cart, then take a ride into the wasteland that England was slowly becoming, due in most part to the ever-virulent bubonic plague that has really made its home here. The journey saddens both Avicia and Paen. They made a stop, admiring a small local church, but heard a rustling, whereupon two dishevelled bodies appeared, looking hard done by. They seemed hard of hearing as

Avicia called out to them. Both totally ignored her shouts and screams. Paen got down off the cart as the thoughtless bodies strolled past him too, oblivious to the fact that he touched both of them. Sensing neither body heat, nor any form of life existence. Unsettling as these lifeless forms wended their way, across the scrub, faceless and an unknown forlorn, without any self-control. Someone or something living or dead had control. The same entity, starting to gain influences, control over external bodies. With the skill, of implanting someone else's thoughts, ideas, mindset. This will be something completely different; needing to find where all this stems from. Fearing that this resurrecting might have been happening for some time.

"I do not think they have any life source, of their own. See if you can delve a little deeper, my wonderful seer," Paen says to Avicia.

"I will try Paen, hold them still for me. I need physical contact."

"Come on down, they are harmless. I have got this one for you. I will hold him while you do your sensing, seeing."

She puts her hands briefly on his head, then his heart, forgetting he did not actually have one of his own. Putting a finger over each of his eyes, penetrating, seeing what he sees. All flashes, of incomplete images, fading thoughts. Strange dark corners hidden from her, hidden presence lurking. Obviously these are the impressions, willed by someone or something else which she cannot see. Producing a new life within an old body, a strong influence indeed, very dark. Especially without any thought, to resurrect a dead body, for a personal use. Paen breaks the neck of the lifeless form held within his hands, whereupon the entity ceases to operate. Lying motionless, expunged, devoid of any motorized energy, at all. The connection with the seer is severed instantly. Paen, catches up with the other body, releasing the energy, by breaking its neck too. Leaving it lifeless on the floor.

"So my wonderful siblys, did you feel something tainted, wobegone! Did you get a presage? Did you see anything, feel anything, sense something out of place, nothing?" Paen spoke out loud.

"Yes I did. But I could not see who or what. But I think we need to search a whole lot deeper, before we are ever likely to find what is behind this. I think Mother would have called it a necromancer. Someone knowingly playing with the dark arts, for his or her own ends. They would seem very capable at it as well. With all the death already around us, it would not be very hard to keep it hidden away," Avicia replies to Paen.

"Then we need to go back to *Riche Mont*, so we can talk to Nefatia. To see if she has ever experienced anything like this before, in her lifetime or a previous existence," Paen responds.

So with a little anxiety, with the insight of Avicia's premonitions, unrelated thoughts and sensory perceptions, from the body probe, she had encountered. They mount the horse and cart, slowly making their way back to the safety, solitude, security of the sisterhoods' home.

Paen tells her, "When we get back, we discuss all this with our sister, the goddess. To see if she can recall any such thing that might help us solve this. Either it is a one-off, or it is going to get bigger; probably so big it will just get out of control. So we need to compile a way forward, to bring all this to a head, to make it crumple as soon as we can."

They both take a slow ride home, letting both their thoughts mull over. But the siblys, trying her best to put everything into some sequence of events. So the journey back was very quiet and uneventful. Avicia was snuggled close to her very own Paen. Finally, on their arrival at the gates, the seer was fast asleep, he was driving the cart during the dimming twilight, as the sun surrenders at the end of the day. Gifting a very rare sunset, as the light pales into insignificance. He had to wake Avicia so she could cast the sign, use the magic word to throw open the gate, so they could enter the forum, with the horse and cart. After dropping the cart, then taking the horse to the stable.

He carries Avicia to her very comfortable bed and covers her, kissing her on her parted lips and fondling her breasts, before leaving her alone. Making his way to his own sleeping pallet, he settles down for the night, hoping to get a long rest so that he is completely refreshed in the morning. So they can explain to the goddess what they came across. Also, what Avicia sought, found with her penetrating the darkest thoughts, of whoever or whatever, the life force, pertaining to the revived body. All is quiet, peaceful, calm; only the plague infiltrates the night. Only the necromancer invades the darkness, revitalizing the dead bodies, or so it would seem. Does guesswork help? Who knows! But something is happening. It is not the carefree world it used to be.

This is new, this raising of dead bodies, for what use? The putrid remains tormented by someone else's wants, needs, desires. Without due respect they are being used by someone, for their own ends, their own gratification. So one way or another, it needs to be halted.

So a very sound night's sleep for everyone. In the morning, naked, Nefatia creeps into Avicia's room lies next to her. To be as close as possible. Avicia could feel her, snuggled close into her. Sleeping together for a little longer. Then Avicia wakes and looks down at the goddess,

“We need to go and see Paen, Nefatia.”

“Let us go to him right away, Avicia.”

Both naked, they march in on Paen as he sleeps, Avicia gently rubs his manhood until he stirs, then awakes.

“I guessed that was you my sweet lady, I could tell by your deft touch.”

“Paen, we need to tell the goddess about our travels yesterday.”

She looks at Avicia, “My beautiful little maiden, you seem to have more than your fair share of mother in you, more than you ever expected. All these abilities, powers, have got stronger, now she has passed on. But you must not let them overwhelm you. Take them and mould them, into your own personal use, so you can interrupt them in your own way.”

“Yes, I know they have got a lot stronger, since Mother died. But it still does not make them any easier to deal with. Especially when I have to use them for a specific purpose. I still have problems sorting them out, what everything means. But I do know when there are deviations, dark corners, things that are being hidden, concealed, hidden away from me.”

Paen is in exactly the same condition as the two women. He works through the day without any clothes so there is nothing to restrict him. Both his admirers sit either side of him as they talk. He lays flat on his back, drifting back off to sleep as the two women talk. But Avicia takes hold of his semi-hard weapon, just letting it lay in the palm of her hand. They both just watch it grow.

“See goddess, most times it is as simple as that. Also the kiss, the same as we always kiss, it works for men too. Go on, kiss him. Mean it like you do when you press against my lips, when we kiss.”

Nefatia leans down, her full red moist lips are hard and tight against his unresisting mouth. Kissing long, desired, feeling the fire in the returned pressure, as he is induced in returning with the same amplitude as it is given. He takes both nipples, softly pulling, twirling, enticing her to sit across his prone body. Avicia, pulling and rubbing his erect organ, making him stand upright and tight against Nefatia's unblemished groin. Always eager for new experiences, the virgin goddess, enthralled and excited by the first touch of a man's body, against her silky flesh. She coyly takes his robust shaft,

"Avicia my love, what do I do next? I feel anxious, hot, bothered, aroused, but as yet, incomplete!"

"Nefatia, now he is hard, he juts into the air. You must mount him. Get him inside you. Sit on him, like a throne."

Avicia rubs and jerks on Paen, keeping him hard.

Nefatia straddles his thick, overpowering, fiery tool as though she is mounting her horse. Then she slides down him smiling and sighing, watching fascinated as he disappears within her aching wanton body. Then Paen bucks, writhes, pushes up, tearing her maidenhead, fully penetrating her nubile, delicious young body.

He is all the way in and she smiling as she feels his surge of rampant heat, his raging urges. Her stunned surprise, on her sensual awakening. Nefatia opens her eyes to find siblys at her side, chewing her exorbitant aroused nipples as she Nefatia rides Paen beneath her.

"Here I was thinking I was dreaming. Instead I find I am mounted by the most trenchant, urbane woman known to man. You stay there goddess, we will finish this together."

"Ingenious Paen, you will have to show me. You are my first man. I was a virgin until a short time ago. Now I am completely yours."

Paen makes sure he is fully inserted into her tight, lavish hairy snatch.

"Are you comfortable, up there on your throne highness?"

"Yes, most comfortable. You are so hot Paen, I can feel you throbbing inside me."

While lying there he rubs, soothes and caresses her big, bountiful breasts. Teasing, pulling her thick and erect nipples. Avicia, pulls and strokes his balls. He pushes up, connecting hard against Nefatia's clitoris. Making her jump, he nearly dislodges her from her erect throne.

"Paen, you nearly knocked me off. Go careful, this is my first time remember. It might be my first time, but I am thoroughly enjoying it. You are thick, long and hard - so rotund. I love feeling you so deep inside me. I just want you to stay as deep as you can. Paen suck my nipples, I love that too. I can tell you are enjoying me."

Once the coupling is completed and all the kissing and hugging subsided, the physical touching of all three has satisfied Avicia, Nefatia and Paen; they turn to the serious business for the day.

"So ladies, shall we go and eat?"

"Yes, Paen. We can tell Nefatia what we saw yesterday, in some detail."

"I would love you, Avicia, to be part of the Sisterhood," Nafatia informs the syblis.

"I would love that too, goddess. I have a feeling this is going to be good for all of us," Avicia smiles as she replies.

"Then let us go and eat, drink and talk," the goddess rises as she talks to Avicia.

"Nefatia, I thought you would be more captious, but you are such a joy to be with and know."

"Paen, once you get to know me, I think after this morning, you will be the first, probably the only man, to really get to know me. Everything all will be so much easier between us."

The three of them sit at the table and partake of a good solid breakfast. Then the goddess offers Avicia a beaker, of clear cool liquid.

"It seems so pure, clean and fresh."

"It holds a single drop of the Elixir of Life. From the supplies my mother gave me. All you need do is drink, for me. Then you will become a Sister within the Sisterhood of Lahmia. Beholden to no one, apart from the sisterhood."

Avicia drinks happily, enjoys. So completely different to anything else, she had drunk before.

"I feel strange, aware, my thoughts more vivid, at one with myself."

"Avicia, my very dear loving sister, it highlights all your attributes, helps you think clearer. It makes you live longer, so you have more time for everything within your life."

"Avicia, Paen, as a daughter of Queen Neferata, I am a vampire. This was given to me by my mother, a birth rite bestowed upon me at my birth as the first daughter, my baptism of blood. Here, let me show you!"

There on the table lay a heart of some animal. Bowing over it, she opened her mouth; then within three bites it was gone. Absorbing, imbibing, the blood, juice, gore. Her eyes turn crimson. Her hair flaring, catching alight; as it turned blood red. Her whole physical appearance, persona awash with blood. As she blossoms to twice her normal size. Avicia petrified, alarmed, scared, clings to Paen. He wraps his arms around her as a protection, shielding her. Slowly the apparition dissipates, the glow lessens. The smell of death evaporates. There, standing before them, is Nefatia, the goddess they both know and love. The woman they thought they knew, yet now holding a new aura for them both.

"So now you know me, the secret I hide from everyone else; except you. Now Avicia, the elixir will not do this to you. It will enhance your own abilities, capabilities, assist you in knowing yourself. So Paen, what have you got to show us? I feel Avicia has never seen you in this form, all the time, she has known you!"

"You are right, in that assumption goddess."

Paen comes out, standing in front of the two women. Closing his eyes; transforming, transcending his human form. There standing on all fours, the lupus albus. A werewolf, so perfectly formed. Masquerading as a lone alpha male. His long, coarse, thick, coat silver grey. The biggest, brightest amber eyes, shining the way for him; like burning coals. Standing as large as a Suffolk Punch. Square, massive, standing on his hind legs; the drool dripping from his jaw. Then just as quick, he was Paen again. Avicia taken aback, lost for words, startled.

"Avicia, Nefatia, do not worry, I knew who you both were. Just because I change, I do not lose my thoughts or reasoning. I know I look powerful; but as I have got older, wiser, I have been able to increase my werewolf transformation. Now we all know each other intimately, I think we need to discuss, what we discovered yesterday; along with your thoughts too, Avicia."

"Now I understand the animal in you, Paen. Why mother and myself, always felt so safe, with you around us."

Then Avicia went on to explain to Nefatia, about their journey outside. How they happened to come across two bodies, that had been dead; but with the aid of someone, or something, they had been able to summon them from the realms of death. Given them the strength, to get up and walk again. She was sure they did not know where they were going, just meandering, until they were stopped by us. It was reckless, but she thought it was probably, the work of a necromancer.

"Avicia, that is not a word that I am familiar with, never heard of it before. So I do not fully understand what you think we are dealing with."

"Goddess, it is someone well practised in the dark arts. Using his knowledge, wisdom and craft to control or take over anything at his behest. With the ultimate power belonging to his master or masters."

"I would think he is using the plague as a cover, to infiltrate some concern that he would like to be in charge of, or take over. Or to promote himself somehow, certainly."

"Why do we need to get involved?"

"Nefatia, we need to stamp it out, to keep the countryside safe. To keep the living alive and the dead in their place of rest. It is not good to have the dead here, unrestricted. What problems will follow if they are not contained?"

"Ladies, between us we will need to find out, how far this has been taken, already."

# CHAPTER EIGHT

Down in the poorly lit undercroft, all alone with his papers, he was busy crafting the incantations needed to work his extremely dark art. He would need three. He had already poured over with the salient points, his bold endeavour. Now he had the charm for the master incantation. He just had to perfect the other two anti-incantations, these gave him the power over other acolytes; which would cover the way the path that was leading to his intent. Towards and against the church for not rewarding him for his allegiance; for all these years. To desecrate the cathedral and to lay the blame at someone else's door. To discredit the man, that should have been exposed long before now; for his insensitivities, exploiting young women, due to his exalted position. Luxuriating himself at the expense of the church, disregarding the needs of his diocese, along with his poverty stricken congregation. Desanctifying the altar of the cathedral. By having sexual relations there, with one of his young, turbulent mistresses. All of this would soon be uncloaked with the help of his human acolytes, with the aid of his dark, devious lord.

The bishop was quite unaware of all this, sat being entertained by his young courtesan. She was trying on some of her lovely dresses, covering her body in these mantles of rare finery. He sat upon his throne naked, and every time he approved of her apparel, she would come over to him, courtesy before him; then climb on him. She would plant his hardness in her, wrap her legs around his back. He would pull her closer still. His eager hands on her tight buttocks he pulled her hot flesh into his hungry groin. Then the two of them, just sat there on the bishop's throne, enjoying the comfort of sex, both dressed in their finest garb.

The Earl along with his Baroness were out for an early morning ride. Just the two of them, quite alone. They come to a halt outside his out-of-the-way hunting lodge. Dismounting, they left the horses to fend for themselves. Entering the well-equipped chamber, the Baroness removes the Earl's codpiece. Without any niceties, the Earl raises her skirt as she bends in front of him. Finding her hot quim, he thrusts himself and his majestic manhood deep within her. It takes her breath away as he copulates, ramming his erect weapon between her wanton loins. Her hands creep around, fondly grasping his manhood, squeezing his heavy balls and wanting him up to his hilt.

He can go no further into her gracious, yielding flesh. The Earl grunts as he pumps, ravishing his lady and exerting all the force he can. He feels her wetness encompass his shaft. She whimpers, wiggles and waggles her opulent behind. He with his hardness bangs, flows and rams himself home. Erupting he ejaculates covering her as well as himself in his torrent of sticky cum.

"Being alone with you, my love, gets me excited. I cannot wait to get you here, then have you straight away."

"I know William. I also want your manhood in me, as soon as I can. Thrust, push - I love your strong, regal rod in as deep as possible, my lord."

So they spend the rest of the day being quite alone. Having long, absorbing sex away from the interruption of everyone else

The archdeacon, on the other hand, finally gets his enchantments and incantations ready. Written and memorized, it is all committed to his memory.

*I call upon you*
*To give my power,*
*To my acolytes.*
*To keep them*
*Empowered*
*For as long as I want*
*Or need.*
*To share until*
*I demand it back*
*In its entirety.*

All he needs now is something from each of his chosen acolytes to have a hold over all of them. To lock them into his personal control and psyche before he can go any further. So he has to pay a visit to the sexton and the priest as well as the deacon. As for the bishop, he was undecided whether to use him or not! But as Gynwell was his first target, he could see no reason why he could not take him under his wing and lead him astray, a little more. Take him in a little deeper than he already is. So the Archdeacon, resolved to start out in the morning, to start collecting the items, he needed for his charm to work.

So looking forward to a good night's rest, because he has lots of riding to do. But just before he does he feels for a connection with the cook's daughter, Malyna. Implanting in her mind that the Earls' niece is coming to visit. She would be worth an introduction to the bishop; first she is of his age preference, his liking. She is attractive, of the age to flirt and deflower, at the

Bishop's convenience. Could be moulded to his liking, perversions. She is still single, as yet never had a man.

John de Offord feels the tie between them, Malyna and the bishop, is still as strong as when he first introduced her to the bishop for the first time. Now all is set, he sleeps ready for the journeying on the following day.

He sets out before the sun rises, alone with his thoughts, not bothered or put out by the fact that the plague is still prevalent all around him. His mission is to obtain the four items, one from each of his unbeknown acolytes. So, off he rides to the priest, to seek him out and gain his confidence; needing only small items, touched at least once, by the aides for the Archdeacon's plan.

The Earl and his lady Godyth were early risers too. They had to be up and ready to receive his niece. She was travelling under escort later that morning. Then they would be off to the Bishop's palace for dinner. Being away from the crowds and court would make a very resting change before he had to go back out into the field, accessing the plague once again. So today was to be enjoyed with his wife, niece and the Bishop.

At the palace, the Bishop was up bright and early. He had already said mass at the cathedral, to his thinning congregation. Now in the kitchen, he was checking all the details for his reception with William de Bohun. Going to the cook, he takes her to one side.

"Mistress cook, pray tell your daughter I will need her company later. Tell her to go to my chamber and choose a dress, as she will be attending the dinner tonight, as company for the Earls' niece. I want her at her finest. Do you understand?"

"Yes your excellency. I will go now, to tell her."

The cook stops what she is doing and rushes out immediately to her own small chamber. Then to her daughter, outside in the market place, selling the vegetables they have managed to secrete away from the kitchen; hidden in her leather scrip. Just to make a couple of extra pennies; to make their life a little more bearable.

"Malyna, when you are done selling, you need to be back at the cathedral. To make yourself splendid, presentable for the bishop. You are to attend the dinner for the Earl, as a companion for his niece. He said to use one of your special dresses for him."

"OK Mother, I will be at my very best. I will come back with you now."

So hand in hand, they wend their way back the palace, the cook back to her toils in the hot, unrelenting kitchen. The young beautiful maiden to the bishop's bedchamber, where she searches through her very own wardrobe. She chooses not her favourite, but the bishop's, which always arouses him. Especially when she raises the hem up to her waist, to show off her cute body. He gets excited, hard, aroused; generally, after that, all the work is done, he is ready for her there and then.

This time she will have to be on her best behaviour. She hides her own clothes behind her wardrobe. Just as she is bending over to loosen her shoes the bishop enters the chamber. On seeing Malyna, he lifts his cassock, rubbing his raised staff. Then, nestling up against her soft flesh, emboldened as he always is, he pushes himself against her round, tight buttocks. Separating her cheeks as he pushes, nudges, "Come on Bishop Gynwell, you are hard, get in me. I want you now, all of you."

He kneels over her, feeling a surge come all over him as he pushes all the way into her very tight orifice.

You're a naughty man, you have cum all over me too. I love all your stickiness, thick goo. Love me until you are finished. I want all of you inside me, for as long as you can give it to me."

"Bless you my child. I love you and your infinitely soft, warm body. Malyna, you always excite me, fulfil me."

"So my glorious bishop, what am I doing for you this evening?"

"The Earl William and his Lady Godyth are coming tonight. They are bringing his niece, with them. I want you to be her companion for me."

"OK, make sure you have finished with me, first. Then we will get ready for our guests."

Losing all his self-control, the Bishop commits himself to the fornicating with his favourite young woman. He cannot help himself as he ejaculates, squirming behind her. Keeping himself fully inserted, the Bishop plays with her tight round breasts as well as her elongated, taut nipples. He lifts her up, as he stands. Takes her to his bed, sitting himself and Malyna, comfortably on his large four poster, he waits patiently as his swollen manhood, retracts. Eventually regaining his normal size, he slips out of her tight, enjoyable body. Getting a handkerchief, he wipes both of them, cleaning as best he can.

"The Earl's niece is your age, Malyna. So you just need to keep her company and amused."

"OK Master Gynwell. Shall we get ready now? I am going to wear your favourite dress. Will that make you happy?"

"My child you are divine, you know me to well. You have always made me happy, so complete. Just give me a minute or two. Then we shall go and receive the Earl and his party."

Having both got dressed, they both go down to the palace gates awaiting the arrival of the Earl of Rutland. The Bishop is the first to step forward looking directly at his lordship. "Welcome William and Lady Godyth. It is good to see you both again and I welcome your niece Amora too."

"Salutations Bishop Gynwell it is our pleasure to be here in your exalted company," William replies.

The Bishop talks further, "come please, make yourselves comfortable after your tiresome journey. Help yourself to the refreshments."

The Earl places in front of him, the young lady who was at his side, "John, this is my niece Amora, I will speak more of her later."

The bishop brings his young courtesan into the company, now explaining, "this is Malyna, a young companion for Amora."

Malyna courtesies smiles and then offers her hand to the young girl. They walk off together towards the main hall.

All is smiles and joy, as they talk, relaying present events that had been keeping them both very busy. Then the Bishop seating his company, ready for the evening together.

As dinner is laid out before them, William de Bohun turns to the Bishop Gynwell, "John, perhaps you can help Godyth and myself."

"With what, William? I may have a solution if you tell me what the problem involves."

"The Baroness and I have to go to London for a while, by wishes from the king. We would like to leave Amora in a safe place, anywhere would be safer than London."

"William, I do have connections at two of our local convents. I am sure the nuns would love the company of a young lady for the duration of your business in the capital."

"That would be very helpful Bishop, do you think you could ask them on our behalf?"

"Of course, we can do that tomorrow."

Then there was a little cough that interrupted the two men's congenial conversation. They all looked up finding Malyna looking and imposing herself upon them all. Bishop John was the first to respond to her remark, "speak child if you have something on your mind, please enlighten us all."

"I do mean to mind my own business. I apologise because I cannot help myself, there is an easier solution, Amora could stay here at the palace under our care and protection, your excellency. I could keep her company and make sure we do not get underfoot. I could show her around although this is not for me to say I know, but Amora could attend the Mass with me on Sundays."

"Malyna, you must not talk out of turn but that would be for the Earl and the Baroness to determine young lady."

Then without another intervention, Lady Godyth turns to her niece asking her directly, "Amora where would you prefer to stay, in the convent full of nuns or here at the Bishop's palace with your new found friend?"

The young lady smiles very openly. Usually she would not have been involved in the conversation at all, but now being consulted and asked for her own personal opinion was something completely different for her. Probably in greater part to the forthright opinion of Malyna, understanding that normally the option of the convent would have been chosen for her without another conversation. The Bishop didn't seem to mind, Malyna would be her confidante. Amora responds with, "Well Auntie Godyth, I would prefer the palace with the bishop and Malyna, but if your heart is set on sending me to a convent then lock me away until you and Uncle William return."

"That is fine child, the palace it is. I pray you behave and do not get under Bishop John's feet, he is a very busy man. Now say thank you to the bishop young lady."

The young lady leaves her seat and approaches John Gynwell and she kisses the ring on his proffered left hand, smiling at him ever so sweetly, “thank you very much, your excellency.”

“You are more than welcome dear Amora.”

Malyna smiles coyly, she knows she has just done the right thing by someone. For the life of her she cannot remember who or where she got the idea from, but it had worked.

Meanwhile, the archdeacon had ridden across the country to visit his friend, Robert Cokerton, to spend some time with him to see how he was dealing with the Black Death. He was wondering if it was going to extirpate the whole of the English population.

He was finding it extremely difficult; grizzly, with so much death. Unable to put a stop to it, his congregation shrinking. He finds it hard to survive himself. The fear of the plague, striking his village, community. Robert himself goes out every day to fend for his village, caring for the weak, disabled, disenchanted and the feeble. The pregnant women are going down with typhoid, as well as the dreaded bubonic catastrophe.

But it made a veritable change for him to have a visitor. He got two beakers, along with a bottle of wine. As they talked late into the night, the archdeacon tells of his exploits, collecting the rents and tythes. The wolf in the forest; the kindness of the mother and daughter feeding them. The Earl makes a fool of himself with the young daughter. Their journey home, with the caitiffs, who they thought were the perpetrators, of the poaching in the forest. Then the night was done, the second bottle of wine was empty.

The archdeacon accepts Robert’s offer for a bed for the night. Both are a little worse for wear, after quaffing a little ale and mead and enjoying both bottles of wine. With these they both retired for the night.

The sun had been up for a while. The archdeacon along with Robert Cokerton both rising very late, the priest gathered together vitals for a breakfast of sorts. Having found some haslet chine with scraps of maslin blessing it all then putting it on the table.

John de Offord finding a button of the priest down in the scullery as they wished each other a fervent good morning. They then sat down to the meal before them quenching their thirst with a jug of ale, reminiscing.

As the meal finishes the archdeacon rises and makes his apologies with promises of another visitation very soon. Then he rides out to see the young deacon who is under his wing. He should get there before nightfall on his trusty spanker.

The Bishop had all his visitors sit at the table. So they could all see the dishes as they were set on the table. The kitchen had prepared chicken and rabbit in almond gravy, herb salad, onion and egg pie, mylates of pork, saffron rice, salmon pie, smoked eel, savoury bread pudding, mushrooms with leeks, grave of small birds. Then the sweet dishes followed: rissole of fruit, apple tostee, pears poached in wine, almond fritters, tartys in apple. Already on the table was ale, mead, cider, small beer, scented with ambergris and raspberries, for the two young girls. Beer spiced with allspice, juniper and cinnamon. Sour wines made from apricots and cherries. The white wines, hyssop, myrtle and Bordeaux.

"All is to be enjoyed and savoured by everyone this evening."

The prolificacy of the reverend bishop was breathtaking. It matched his dissipation, if only they had known him better. The banquet set before them did not stop the idle chatter, the drinking and the getting to know each other a little better. The adults talked of the shattered lives and communities across the county. Due to the, uncontrollable spread of the very damaging Black Death, along with the upsurge of typhoid. Both disseminating, restricting work, due to the number of deaths, it had caused within the county.

The two young ladies, seemed to be getting on very well, talking of this and that. Her time spent with John Gynwell had broadened her horizons and her knowledge, so Miss Malyna felt quite at home with the Earl's niece.

Eating and drinking a little mead, and William thinking of the thankless task he has of going back across the county, checking on his sheriffs. Before he set out to London, to council with Edward III.

The Bishop shows his guests to their chambers, wishing them all a very good night's sleep. He tells his favoured courtesan, that she will have to take to her own bed tonight, because of the company they have here at the palace. He would see her in the morning, for the departure of Earl William and the Baroness Godyth. She smiled happily - a free night! That does not happen very often. A blessed night of sweet, rapturous sleep resting her tired, unfortunate body. So the palace was at rest, as the kitchen comes to a rest as well. Everyone is at home in bed. But daylight comes around far too quickly.

The kitchen comes back to life with breakfast at the ready, eaten. All too soon, with their guard, personal escort, William de Bohun and his Lady are on their way back home. Their niece waves adieu, alongside the Bishop and the young Malyna. With a backward glance there was a shout of goodbye from her uncle, William, followed by a wave from her unseated aunt, Godyth. They disappear with their score into the late morning sun. Once they are out of sight, gone over the horizon, John Gynwell avails himself to his new ward.

"Young lady, would you like me to show you around the palace and the cathedral?"

"Bishop, you could show me to my chamber first. It would please me so."

"Come then ladies, let me show you. Then Malyna can help you move your wardrobe. Perhaps avail yourself of some of her dresses, I can put them at your disposal as you seem to be of the same size. Perhaps you may need more changes than you have managed to bring along with you? Malyna, show Amora to the chamber next to yours. So you can keep an eye on her, show her where everything is?"

"Of course Bishop Gynwell, we will see you later, perhaps?"

"Yes, we will see each other. But I need to go and change."

The Bishop had heard his name being called. His attendance was required on some local matter, so he left the two young ladies to their own devices. Malyna called on two of the Bishop's servants to give them a hand to move Amora's wardrobe to her very own chamber. They laid it all out, putting it away. Then Malyna took the Earl's niece through to the Bishop's chambers.

"Here are the dresses you can use, if the fancy takes you, Amora. They are mine for now."

"They are very pretty, Malyna. But why are they in the Bishop's apartment?"

"When it is just the Bishop and me. He lets me wear them, providing no one else is around. But no one else knows, so that is why he keeps them in here."

"I see he gets lonely, in this large place!"

"Yes, I think he does. It is his way of sharing, when I spend time alone with him. I think I can hear him coming, let's go into our quarters, until he's ready."

She opens the interconnecting door, both disappear into the adjoining chamber.

The Bishop lays the papers on his desk, wanting terribly to get out of his bishop's regalia into something a little more comfortable, less formal. He removes it all, putting it away, hanging in his closet. Finding something more to his liking, far less official, he lays it on his bed. He freshens up with some cool water, dries himself, lays on his bed and falls asleep beside his clothes.

Having had a catnap, he feels so much better for it. John Gynwell rises naked just as the interconnecting door opens wide. The two young ladies enter, the niece thoroughly embarrassed; turning red she blushes profusely. Hiding her eyes and she looks down instantly. Malyna is not put out at all.

"Your Excellency, our apologies. We did not know you were here. We just came to get a dress. Can we help you in any way?"

"I was just about to get dressed, then do some work. You could get my clothes for me."

"Of course."

She goes to the other side of the bed to fetch the Bishop's clothes, then brings them round to him so he can dress himself.

"Have you never seen a naked man before, child?"

"No, your excellency. Is it a sin to see you like this, unclothed?"

"No young lady. There was no ill intent. You will have to excuse me, I am getting quite aroused with you standing there, looking at me. You being so beautiful, as well."

"Thank you Bishop, for saying I am beautiful. No one has ever told me that before. But should I go? I am not sure what to do! You do look excited. He looks vexed, hard, hot."

"No need to go. Come here, feel him. Then you need not be so bashful, coy, the next time you see a naked man."

The niece abashed as the Bishop goes to her, standing before her. Amora dazzled by his encroaching manhood. But the cook's daughter, Malyna takes her hand, placing it on his sac, gently squeezing his strangely shaped gonads. Then, putting her thumb and forefinger at the top of his raging staff, he gets her to squeeze, grip his hard, austere, round pole. Then he shows her the up and down movement, along his throbbing length. At last he tells her, "Just copy me. Do as I do, to make the Bishop a whole lot happier."

Malyna plants a big juicy kiss on the shiny red dome. The niece bends her head to kiss, a gratifying gentle kiss; but instead lets the crown slip in between her sweet, virginal lips. She sucks as she pulls away; his eye emits a little secretion. Amora pushes her tongue out, licking the white, sticky sediment away.

"That was rather naughty, young lady!"

"Yes, I know. But I have never been left on my own before. I feel rather adventurous. But if I do anything wrong, or incorrect, I am sure either you or Malyna will put me right."

"Did you enjoy his excellency's erect manhood?"

"Yes, it seemed to get so much harder when I took hold of it. Longer, when I had it in my warm mouth."

"Yes, my cute Amora. That is the way to excite and enthral a man."

"Bishop Gynwell, can I do it again for you?"

"I need to do some work. You can come back later, with Malyna tonight and if you would like to. Play with him then."

"I would love to see you tonight. But he is so hard and eager now. Please let me finish him now. I am sure you would like me too, wouldn't you?"

"OK my child. I will lay down. Malyna will show you how to finish me and satisfy me, young lady."

The bishop lays back in the bed, naked, erect and throbbing. His young courtesan takes hold of his pulsing staff. Gripping it in between her well-practised hands and fingers; she with an open mouth, slides down his hard length; taking him all in, filling her mouth with his eager rod. Then up, stopping at his bulbous, shiny crown. Licking it with the tip of her voracious tongue.

"Amora, just do that, until he explodes all over you. Unless you can swallow quickly. It is creamy, thick and sticky, but it will not hurt you in any way."

The two young ladies exchange places. The young, beautiful niece copies all of Malyna's movements. As well as sucking, she tightens her grip around the top of his shaft. Strokes him as her mouth comes up towards the top. She can feel his tension, pressure; she ready for him. She pushes the tip of her tongue directly into the eye of his swollen red tip. He cannot help himself as he ejaculates. She drinks him dry; some of the spoils on her hands, but she licks that away. Amora is perspiring, hot yet happy and smiling, "So my over-ripe Bishop, how did I do, for my first time with you?"

"That, young lady, was amazing, I loved every single touch and stroke. If you still want to come later, you are more than welcome to my bed."

“Try stopping me Bishop, now I have the taste for you. I really enjoyed your hard pole. It filled my mouth with your thick, sticky cream.

# CHAPTER NINE

The archdeacon was close to the church where the new deacon, was practising his newfound calling. Using the big black knocker on the Towering church door, the noise reverberated through the whole auditorium. At last the Dean finally appeared to answer the call.

"John de Offord, it has been a while. A pleasure to see you after all this time. Do come in. Let me take your coat. Come and join us for supper."

"Thank you kindly, Adam."

So very courteously he sat joining the merry throng. He knew the parish priest, as they both acknowledged each other. Then the deacon speaks up, "Just a couple of moments of your valuable time if you would be so kind. First of all, I would like to introduce you to our beloved archdeacon, John de Offord, for those that do not know him, who has surprised us with a personal visit."

Then he turned to the archdeacon, "I would like to introduce our parishioners, or perhaps I should say the remnants, of our once very active community to you."

"So, our young boy has now become a public speaker. So how has this come about?"

"Well John, the harvest has been poor. The fields devastated by the lack of attention, due to the spread of typhoid, alongside the dreaded plague. So once a week, we invite our dwindled parish to dine with us, here. The speaking has just helped me to get to know my villagers, I feel good when I stand up and suggest ways of helping one another, just talking generally to them."

"That is a lovely idea, does everyone come?"

"Yes, most times. If someone does not make it on our communal evening, then we go and check up on their situation."

"That is one way of keeping a check on your parishioners and their welfare, good for you."

So they partake of the bread and other vitals on the table before them. Then as evening turns to night, they slowly leave. Wending their way home, they look forward to another day in the morning.

John de Offord acquires a small stud from the deacon's garment as he sees off his parishioners into the night. Again he accepts a bed for the rest he requires before his long ride back home, to Lincoln. After a good night's sleep and rest and a simple breakfast, he says his goodbyes to the deacon. He reclaims his horse from the stables, making his way back towards the cathedral. Just a slow, gentle ride, through the countryside. There are two more articles to collect, then he can get on with the more important stuff, as a necromancer.

John Gynwell, having spent the afternoon working on some formal papers and documents, stretches in relief as a soft, gentle knock on the connecting door. With a smile he replies, "Come my children."

The door opens, and two servile young maidens enter his chamber, "Shall we go for a walk around the cathedral, or even my palace, my very dear young ladies?"

Amora smiles her sweetest smile, dressed in a very fetching full-length dress, "It is late my dear Bishop John. Could we do the tour tomorrow, when we have a full day?"

Malyna blows the bishop a kiss and replies with, "The Earl's niece wants to learn more about a man's body."

"My dear, beautiful girl, to do that, she must know her own body. First does she know her own body all that well?"

"Bishop, Malyna, I probably do not know my body at all. In fact I have never experienced anything with this sweet body of mine ever. No one has ever shown me. My body is quite normal, nothing exceptional. Not sure of the subtleties, not sure I ever will know. But I want to learn . Would you, Malyna, help me?"

While she waited for a reply, his little favourite explained to him that he would help her. Because she had already told Amora what the two of them got up to, when they were alone. The niece was shocked at first, but then warmed to the idea when Malyna told her, she could learn and partake of the instruction he would give her.

"OK my little virgin. We will help you know your body as well as a man's. So first you must remove your dress. Then lay on the bed for us."

Amora modestly removes her dress, as well as her other garments. She is not sure what to do next as the reverend John Gynwell just looks at her untarnished body. Then he kneels in front of her, twirling her little pink nipples, then kissing both of them. He then stands up, slowly disrobing in front of this bashful, modest maiden. Naked in front of her, he takes her warm, very soft hand and places it on his erect, rampant staff.

"Do you remember what you did last night, to me? How you enjoyed it so?"

"Yes Bishop. Now can I suck you again?"

"Of course my pretty girl. Remember first we must discover your body. Then you can enjoy the man's, even more so."

The niece kisses his hard shaft. She grips his pole, rubbing it and feeling him stiffen even more, whilst under her care.

"Now young lady, let me pick you up, then lay on the bed."

As he picks her up, he rubs his manhood against her fresh, willing loins. He lays her on her back, kneeling over her, and casts his organ in between her taut, plump breasts. Folding her ample bosom over his energetic, expanding hardness, with a slow rhythmic motion he makes love to her two virginal orbs.

"Amora, rub your fingers over my exposed, scarlet head when you can see it. Do you like the feeling? I know I do."

"I love the feeling of my flesh against your thick, blue-veined shaft. Both with my fingers here. As well as your hefty organ against my sweet breasts."

"Now I am going to leave in you in the hands of Malyna. She knows her body inside out. She will show you all the hotspots on your untainted body. Once you get those, then we can get you playing with a man's body, inside and out. Then there is the play of both bodies, together, which is the final pleasure."

"Well Bishop, let's start, then I can get to know your body, even better than I do already."

"Amora, if you are sure it is my body you want, desire first!"

"It is, because you started me on this journey. So I want you, to be the one that takes my virginity. I want you to be my first man, inside of me. To turn me from a girl to a woman."

A servant knocked on his chamber, "Your excellency, the archdeacon is here to see you."

"Thank you, tell him I am on my way."

Turning around, he retrieved his clothes and got dressed, "My apologies ladies. Please excuse me. I will be back as soon as I can. I am sure you can amuse each other, while I am away."

Walking to his lounge he sat in his favourite chair, "Good evening Bishop Gynwell."

"Good evening to you, Archdeacon. How are you?"

"I am very well, thank you for asking. I have just had a busy couple of days. The new dean is doing a very good job, with his new diocese. There are quite a few parishes languishing, struggling with the conditions at the moment. Perhaps we need to combine some, because of the destitute and dwindling population."

The Bishop John Gyngell smiles agreeing as he replies, "That could be a good plan, also cut down on the number of priests we need too, in these very trying times. We can discuss that soon. Was there anything else?"

"No Bishop, I will leave you to your letters."

They both nod to each other, the archdeacon has acquired a quill while waiting for his excellency. So there is only the sexton to see now. That can wait until the morning.

The Bishop makes his way back to his chamber. On opening the door, he sees Malyna on top of Amora in the sixty-nine position. Both heavily into each other, both licking, slurping at those tender, volcanic Venus mounds. Each is enjoying the other to their fullest extent.

John Gynwell helps himself, as he joins in. He plays with all four tantalizing nipples in turn. Pulling, twisting and twirling, he rubs with the tips of his fingers. Caressing and stroking, he massages those four fabulous breasts at his complete disposal as the two young maids were busy licking at their juices as they flowed from between those four, thrashing legs. John's ministrations helped the flow with his wise, gentle touches.

The Earl William called to the King's council, alarmed at the shortage in labour across the whole country. Livestock was dying where it stood. Crops were rotting in the fields, because no one was available to do the harvesting. The general abandonment of the whole structure of life, living and the welfare of everyone was at stake. Everything was failing, falling apart because the commoner was refusing to work. An uprising was in the forefront of not only country life, but all life across England. A revolt was on its way. His Liege Lord wanted it stopped before it started. The shout for increased wages, for more labour was heard. But was increasingly being ignored, at some vital cost to the economy.

So the Earl made his way to London, with his Lady Godyth, under his own personnel escort.

The Archdeacon praying for continence, with the sexton. Both affable, they drink freely as they ate the smoked eel, stuffed chine and the haslet that the Archdeacon had provided. He had secured a button from the sexton's coat. So he was free and easy in the man's company for the rest of the evening.

The Bishop left a love bite, his mark, on the young vulnerable niece's neck. Kissing her gently on her fragrant, soft lips, he kissed her all the way down her supine, soft neck, guiding her hand onto his stiff rod.

"My dear, rub him slowly, he will show his appreciation, I can assure you."

So the niece rubs, strokes and rolls, revealing his red glowing tip. She runs her thumb over his swelling, glossy, head. While she plays with him, he is sucking her nipples, making them erect and sturdy.

"Do you find this enjoyable, my delicate, fine young woman?"

"Yes John. I tingle all over. I feel hot, excited, something I cannot seem to control."

"That is as it should be. Now, just part your legs for me Amora."

Bishop Gynwell slowly licks her labia, so daintily as to make them swell. Then pushing his tongue between them, he makes her squirm.

"I am going to turn on my back. I want you to sit on my face."

"OK Bishop, I will. Tell me when I am in the right place."

He turns as she sits above him, "Amora, that is perfect."

Wriggling, not protesting as his tongue darts all over her virginal quim, Malyna jumps on the bed and takes hold of John's rigid pole. Rubbing her hands up and down his full length, she takes him into her mouth. She sucks gloriously, taking all of him. She loves his saltiness as she squeezes his full sac and gonads. Feeling herself get a little wet, she ceases the sucking and instead climbs aloft his firm, stout rod, slides down, holds onto Amora's waist; as she manipulates his tool for her maximum pleasure and enjoyment. She changes the position of her hands as they close over her dear young friend's breasts. She runs her fingertips, around and around her smooth, fine aureoles and queezes her taut, upstanding nipples between her enchanted fingers. Then taking hold of her bosom, one in each hand she squashes and pulls, caressing softly.

Determined to splinter her unspoilt hymen, the Bishop rubs her vigorously with his middle finger, feeling it give a little.

"Malyna, I am about to take young Amora here, she is ready. Amora, my beauty, turn around. Now you see where Malyna sits all pretty and happy. I want you sitting there, comfortable and ready."

"Ooooohhh, John that looks almighty big for me, are you sure?"

"Let Malyna help you, my dear. Take it slowly. Take your time, just ease me in, until you are satisfied and not uncomfortable."

"Come Amora, just watch me and how I do it."

Malyna kneels over the Bishop, holding his upright unbending staff. She puts it between her legs and sits on him, sliding down his loving member.

As she dismounts from the Bishop, Malyna tells Amora, "Now you try. Let me guide you, as you mount, then sit on his throbbing pole." The niece straddles the Bishop, holding onto his shaft, while Malyna parts her delicate pink love lips.

"You need the bulbous, shiny crown resting against you there. Now just slip down. Enjoy, dance on him."

The niece slithers, stops.

"Bishop, Malyna what is stopping me from going any further?"

"It is only your tight maidenhead. Let me push up slowly."

"Ooooohh, no stop, oohh!"

"Be patient dear."

A quick surgical lunge up and the Bishop was home and in.

"Oh, that is a lot better. Finally I have you right inside me. My first man. It feels good. Nearly too big for me. So thick, hard and long. I can feel you throbbing," She says in short, uneven gasps.

"My glorious, beautiful lady, now you need to ride me. Slowly, go up and down, then speed up once you are moist.

Eventually you will get carried away with yourself. Then just go as fast as you can, the pleasure will follow I assure you, Amora."

She jiggles at first, adjusting her position. Getting comfortable just as the Bishop lunges up, straight in on her downward stroke. Malyna helps her get comfortable, more reassured in her sitting position. John in the meantime, pummels her lovely, tight, pink pussy. She starts cumming, her juices flow, making it far easier for both the Bishop and the delightful Amora to have sex. John Gynwell holds her down tight, on his thick, rampaging rod, "My glorious young woman, hold on, I am just about to ejaculate. You will feel my heat, my stickiness, spread across your whole sensitive body."

He explodes, drenching her in his liquid love, inside and out. She overflows with him.

"I am no longer a virgin. Bishop, you are my first man. I enjoyed was pleasured by every inch of your juicy manhood."

"You my loving, very dear Amora, were the perfect, untried virgin. You made me cum so much. It must have been your extremely tight, passionate quim. We must do it again, before you leave. Would you both like to join me in my bed tonight?"

Excited at the very thought, the Earl's niece stays atop the Bishop, "Yes I would. I think I am going to stay here, until you shrink for me, my wonderful John."

Malyna smiles and climbs onto the bed. They kiss long and passionately as she snuggles close into his secure arms.

By now the archdeacon is safely back in his office with his four items from his loyal if unbeknown acolytes locked away in his vaults until the following morning Then his bid to change his life, will start with a vengeance. Everyone has had a good night's rest.

The Archdeacon gets dressed very quickly, wanting, needing to get down the vaults as soon as possible. He needs to convert his incantation, into Latin for it to work coherently. With his research and passion, he cannot get to his papers soon enough. He has his incantation in English. He spends the best part of the day translating it, correctly, into Latin.

The Earl sits in the King's council discussing the state of the country, the economy, the increased price of labour and the rising prices of food. The blight of the plague has taken a strong foothold within the country, along with an insurgence, to epidemic proportions, of the latest outbreak of typhoid. Between them they are weakening every structure that upholds the very strength of England.

John Gynwell awakes shrouded by the two warm bodies of the genteel women. One his favoured courtesan, the other the Earl's very own niece. They both sleep, with the niece's hand cradling his semi-erect organ; gripping it, unwilling to let it go anywhere else. Malyna's head is up against John's, the Bishop's hand cupped over her muff, caressing her with his eager fingers. Feeling her gyrate as he strokes her intentionally, his finger penetrates and leaves itself there. Laying naked, he makes himself pulsate and throb as he thinks of where his finger lies at this precise moment in time. Feeling her squeeze him, as he grows within her little hand, the Earl's niece awakes, going beneath the covers to eat the Bishop's quaking manhood before it is totally wasted. Malyna gyrates on the thick digit of Bishop John: wet, eager and wanton and completely aroused by him she throws the covers back. The niece looks up and lets go as her dear friend climbs on top of him. Taking all of him she just sat there, gorging on his staff. Amora at his side, she takes his middle finger, pushing it between her young, nimble, supple loins. She can now feel him sampling her delights with his long, chubby finger. They kiss small single kisses all getting very comfortable in each other's company.

Malyna slips along his thick girth, smiling at her pleasure and the joy she gives John.

"My dear young lady, I think we should give Amora a go as well, don't you think?"

"Yes John."

The archdeacon's translation complete, he goes to his vaults to collect his four primary objects. He sits in front of his incantation with the four objects sat on the parchment.

Then slowly, silently the incantation started! It Reverberated around his crypt, echoing more the louder he got. Until finally he was on his feet, loud and in control. Taking the power within himself he absorbs the surge coursing through the atmosphere. The four items hovering, dematerialising; eventually being absorbed within the parchment they were sat upon. Locked in, all part of the necromancers' contract. Now the inane power, electricity, trying not to let it overwhelm him.

The parchment is now part of his very own altar. The power is all his, at his immediate command. His soul is now owned by his dark creator, the spirit which led him along this very devious, creative, volatile path. A culmination of so many variants, he senses his creation going forth. Rich, vibrant excelling itself, gaining the very life force it was intended for; it needed to survive.

The Archdeacon uses other external forces which would soon be on their way.

Having spent most of the night thinking about the pressures, put upon the King. How best to subvert the possible uprising against him. His ideas he would put before Edward in the morning. But now at this late hour he needed to be in bed, attending his beautiful wife, Godyth. Disrobing in the ante-chamber he walked into his bedroom in all his glory, where his disenchanted wife sat up, her eyes nearly popping out of her head, "William, what a splendid sight. I can see you are excited to see me. Come to me this minute, so I can feel how hard and powerful he is."

He comes to her side. She runs her long delicate fingers up and then down his enraged, blue-veined organ. Godyth loved feeling his large shaft, in her hands. As he stood there, completely under her control she put him in her wide open mouth. Sucking hard long on him, deep, to the back of her throat she tastes the salt, the vigour of the hot flesh enjoys the slow profusion of sauce that followed.

William de Bohun exposes his wife's' firm, full, glorious round breasts and caresses them softly, pulling and tweaking her large, robust, red nipples. The physical contact makes his manhood rise, more eager to flourish. Godyth adept at playing with his shaft, knowing the signs; she runs her thumb over his delicate, red dome. Smiling, she knows what his urgent, jerking movement meant. Closing her nimble mouth around him, she drinks all his milk, as he squeezes her large, ripe, erect nipples. Unable to control himself, under his wife's practiced ministrations. Still hard and stiff, she climbs out from her warm covers. Removing all her night clothes, she kneels on all fours, still on the marital bed. Her mature body still excels at making him want her badly.

Her rampant husband climbs onto the bed, getting in close behind her very willing and receptive body. Rubbing his upright, throbbing manhood against her soft, mellow buttocks, still sticky, softly pushing himself into her tight derriere. His oval crown slipped into her irresistible delights. Taking his whole length, she enjoys the fact he has kept his erection even though he has cum once already, very unusual for him. He happy to be able to continue enjoying his wife, he gently rides her firm, warm, giving rump. Both enjoy the rhythm of his tender motions. He especially her tightness, wrapped around his enraged manhood.

"My voracious, glorious Godyth, you still astound me after all these years. Are you ready for me now?"

"Yes, my dearest William. I want you immediately. My breasts need your loving too, I want your pole there first."

"Lay on your back, my heavenly sweetness, your desires will be answered."

Godyth looks up at him. He kneels over her, placing his robust, unflinching organ in between her mighty heaving bosom. She wraps her full round orbs over his bloated, tensile manhood. Driving backwards, forwards flesh against flesh. Enflamed, her breasts on fire; his raging staff burning, nearly beyond his own self-control. But he promised to love her bosom; he loves every inch of his wife's fabulous torso. He relishes all physical contact with her, so everything they do together is a delight, an unexpected pleasure. Desiring her a lot more often than he can actually have her, he always takes his time when they are alone and making love.

He withdraws from her excellent breasts, making her lay on her side. Entering her quim from behind, he lays with her in his secure arms, pulling her to him, fully inserted as deep as he can be. Gently throbbing inside her, he locks into her as she squeezes her warm, soft, malleable thighs together to keep him in place. With a gentle rocking motion, he agitates himself and his beloved wife. Both enjoy the full insertion, just waiting for the explosive, carnal sensation that William always ends with. But he tries to make sure his wife is satisfied too, tries to make her climax before he does, otherwise she has lost her chance to fully enjoy their exploits together. Godyth grunts as William causes friction by pumping long hard strokes into her. Now she now feels her juices flow, just waiting for him! When he arrives, he hugs his wife tightly. He cums, a thick steady stream of his white cream. She forces herself back onto him, wanting to enjoy all that he can give to her. Slowly they fall asleep, naked together in each other's arms. In the throes of ecstasy. A great night of sleep; giving him a clear mind, a body full of energy.

Godyth slept on while William rose and got dressed before then going to attend, his liege lord, King Edward III.

# CHAPTER TEN

Mephitic! His whole character has changed. The phantasm crept into him, bestowing such strange influences and images upon his very active optic nerve. Dark dreads, voids of despair, overcame and sunk him. Down on his knees, the soul destroyer crushing him completely, from above. The creature was awoken by the necromancers personal invoke. Behemoth entered, rippled through his own now weak vessel, eating his very soul and shredding it through barbed, razor-sharp incisors. The pain had numbed and could not be felt, because it happened so quickly. After a while the archdeacon slowly redeemed himself. Regaining a sense of self; where there was an I, now occupied by five. The priest, the sexton, the deacon, all alongside the bishop and the new Archdeacon. All fighting to gain control, but the might of John de Offord was in there, rising to the top. His abstinence from all things immoral, no diversions, his drive for self-countenance had won through.

He could feel the pull, the meanness, the toxicity of power, the strength to crush and annihilate. To transfer his life stream to something inert. Totally dead and by a single thought or whim, the ability within to give it life, no matter how long it had been dead. With all five conscious working in conjunction with one another to reform and reactivate the five mortals, back into the world of the living. He stood before his altar, breathless. His eyes devoid of any colour. His body has become a furnace of black heat. A heat not from hell but from beyond, created long before the age of man. Now it was the resource of a single deity or entity. He waved his hand; his four acolytes, now under his deliverance and, sheer force of will.

They would share his burden, until he had what he wanted. With a single thought five bodies, once presumed dead, their lives expired due to the blight of the plague, now rise at his call with no other function than to do this one man's bidding.

# CHAPTER ELEVEN

The priest cut short his Sunday sermon and left his pulpit. To hold his own countenance, within the confines of his own office. His congregation is left at a loss as what to do with his disappearance. They sit there hoping for his return, but it not very forthcoming finally, they disperse and make their way home far earlier than any other Sunday morning, they can ever remember.

The Sexton is single, beholden to no one. Deliberating, pondering his accounts, for the week he stops, rises and locks his door. Then sits back down, lost in the wilderness of his mind. He finds himself lost in thoughts, suggestions that do not seem to be wholly his at that particular time.

The dean, having taken the very early Mass. Partaken of his breakfast, having just read the parable of the Good Samaritan. Then, closing the Bible, along with his eyes, he succumbs to the power of the archdeacon.

The Bishop is enjoying the early attentions of both Amora and Malyna. The niece squeezes him hard and long with her warm, tight loving pussy. She has caught him on the rise with an early morning erection. Just beginning her bouncing action, she hopes he will last. But no, he ejaculates far too early.

"Amora, I am sorry, please forgive me."

"I forgive you John, I should have waited for you, to get a little more settled, harder. I will try again later. Let us sleep, for now."

Bishop John turns to help Amora dismount. She faces him as he sucks on her virulent pink nipples, enjoying her vitality and youthful sweetness. In the meantime, Malyna's hands toy with Amora's agitated quim, is turning her attentions to John's manhood. The Bishop thought it a complete and utter joy not to have to sleep alone, to have companions of the opposite sex in his bed. He enjoyed all the attention and, to his knowledge, he had managed to keep it a secret. So only Malyna, her mother and now Amora knew about it. Malyna worked on John de Offord, making him upright, buoyant and thick where the young Amora had failed. First slipping her warm, wet lips over his expanding dome, she licked at his saltiness. He lay on his back, his readiness now showing. Not waiting for him to awaken, she just went ahead, helping herself. Climbing over him, she mounted his obvious hardness, thickness. First she sat astride him, like a young queen upon her royal throne. She leans forward, then down, poking her little tongue out, licking the tip of his nose, eyelids and along the lips of his mouth. Her hands gripped his thighs as she starts to writhe, wriggle and gyrate on his surging organ.

Feeling him thicken and lengthen while his blue veins pulse, she squeezes her hot, lithe loins together to fully appreciate this devilish old man within the confines of her own curvaceous, unholy vessel. She pulls on her own surging nipples, able to reach and suck on them herself. At last she stokes the Bishop's dreams! But at last she satisfied, wet as her juice flows over them both. Now she pays more attention and pumps a little harder, feeling him quiver and throb, his shaft banging against her swollen clitoris. Now she is really agitated, wanting more from Mister Gynwell who lies beneath her. She pulverizes his resolute organ, slamming against him on her hard, downward strokes. Malyna shudders again as she feels herself climaxing, yet again. Another sticky cascade as her love juice, as her thick cream finds its own escape route. Leaning backwards she fiddles, finding his heavy sac and squeezes softly, long, as his erect and heaving tool ploughs her soaking wet furrow. She urges him to sow his seed, deep into her very obliging, fertile quim, "Oh my goodness, I thought I was only dreaming."

The Bishop is now wide awake, now surging, pushing up into the delights of the young Malyna and grating against the soft, delectable, durable walls of her loving vagina.

Amora, now awake too is kissing John hard on his lips; then she rises to Malyna's torso. Drawing her erect, hot nipples into her mouth she sucks hard, feeling the vibrant cherries grow instantly as she caressed them with her eager tongue.

He pressures himself to cum in slow rough strokes as his endeavour starts to pay dividends. Plundering his beautiful courtesan, "Malyna, you ride me like a horse! My staff burns, even though he is deep inside you."

"Then cum for me John. I want your seed. Then I shall stop riding you so hard and so fast. I will dismount you, like a young lady. Until then, I will ride you like a young wench, a harlot determined to get her own way in affairs of the heart."

"My lady Malyna, then allow me to satisfy your devilish desire, my manhood is all yours."

She stops her pounding and rises off him, "Amora, tease the Bishop's shiny crown, please."

"Yes Malyna, it would be a joy."

She traces her nimble finger tips all over, across his opulent red dome. Running her thumb up, then down his pulsating blue vein. Squeezing his full sac, even putting him into her hot, eager mouth, she sucks him hard and long until traces of his saltiness appeared. They both hear him grunt and quake, his erect rod quivering. Amora moves out of the way; Malyna reseats herself upon his rock-hard manliness. She adjusts herself, then slowly forces herself down his entire length. Reaching the hilt, he explodes! She squeezes her slim legs together to keep his organ, as well as his lusty white juice, within her own wanton, craving body.

"Bishop! There, I knew you could do it. I just want that to happen a lot more often, do you hear?"

"Yes Malyna, I promise you will have every time from now on."

"I want you so excited, you lose complete control, for me and Amora too, do you understand?"

"Yes Malyna. Whether it is you or Amora, you shall both have me, each and every time from now on. I will satisfy your own personal needs. You can both enjoy me, have your own way. But now you will have to wait for my swelling to go down, my very dear child, before you try to climb off me."

"Your excellency, you are big. I can sit her all day. But I think Amora deserves you now."

So the sweet young Amora climbs on, replacing her friend. Taking the bishop into her, she relaxes and enjoys what she had missed from the night before. Both young ladies are satisfied and happy, enjoying the Bishop just as much, perhaps even more so now than his excellency just enjoyed them. Amora squeezes her thighs, milking John until he had finished and his swelling subsided. She climbed off him, kissing him once again, both smiling when the Bishop rose.

Then all of a sudden the Bishop, escorting both of the young attractive maidens to the niece's room, locks the connecting door. Then he lays back onto his own bed, looking to all and sundry, as though he is fast asleep.

# CHAPTER TWELVE

Paen wakens, feeling like a thorn between two roses as he looks both sides of him, where lie Avicia and Nefatia. They had decided that between them there was a need to check daily, outside Riche Mont to see if the situation had worsened. Or if they had just imagined the two bodies. If they had not, then there was a need to investigate. View the crisis, see if there was a problem, then either how to counteract it, or view it with suspicion, then find out who the culprit was, or is. Then to find out what he or she is after.

This is where the hard work starts; trying to establish who is at the forefront of these macabre deeds, and where they work from. But first trying to discover a focal point, somewhere to gain a foothold. To attempt to disassemble the seething undercurrent, of claiming the dead for their own end, whatever that may be.

Paen is up and before reaching the door; uncloaked snarling and scales the fence as though it was not even there. As the shadow transforms into his werewolf psyche, he bounds into the woods at an amazing speed, back to where they found their first two rejuvenated mortals. Sensing an imbalance ahead of him he slows, comes to a halt. He finds himself watching a pauper's grave, still uncovered. There three bodies are attempting to claw their way out, of the collapsing pit where they would have been buried, this coming morning. He checks that no one else can see him or is standing close by in this moist, misty open zone. He goes forward, crawling on his belly, sniffing and smelling death, decomposition. Then violently, without a second thought, he snaps at their rotting throats. The provicator subduing their attempts at escape. With three severed throats, their heads loll backwards, falling back, unable to stop the reaction, into the grave from where they came. Now they are just inert, waiting patiently to be buried along with all the others. Silent Shadow with a gut wrenching sprint, stopping for no one or anything but heads home at full tilt, towards his two fancies. Wanting, needing to share desperately what he had encountered. The futility of the dead. What he did to counteract its forward momentum. To physically desecrate the body, so it is of no further use to the controller. Obviously his powers do not extend to the living, which is very fortunate for the rest of the populace.

Godyth welcomes her husband home from another extended day with the King and his undecided council. Still not able to come to terms with his country that is beginning to fall apart. Leprosy was abundant, on top of typhoid and the Black Death. The susceptibility of man against filth, waste, uncontrollable sewerage and flowing through narrow streets. The spread of disease, pollution and livestock waste fouling rivers, streams. There is unclean water everywhere.

The King was no nearer a solution, as William in his favourite position with the amorous Godyth. Takes her from behind. Enjoying the tight closeness of full penetration. He kisses the back of her supine neck he caresses her full, plump breasts. Running his fingers round and round again her uneven, sensitive aureoles. Again he pulled and twisted her erect, hard nipples. In the process he makes himself more erratic, prolonging, increasing his erection, thicker, harder as he plays with his loving wife.

Paen bounds over the high wall. As he falls to the other side, he lands on his own two feet. Casually he walks into his chamber. The two celestial beauties that are Nefatia and Avicia are still fast asleep, abound in their silent serenity. He does not want to impose on them!

Then thinking of what he had experienced, he kisses both of them on their partially opened lips. When that has no immediate effect, he kneels down between them, softly licking their pink muffs. Gradually both women start tossing, turning; moaning, their languid positions changing to ones of submission, yet of pleasure. With Avicia he toys with her eager pussy, rubbing her with his middle finger. Then with Nefatia, he caresses her squirming loins with the flat of his thumb, continuously. Smiling, he keeps this up until at last they both awake.

They rub their eyes with one hand, the other going in between their legs to see what was arousing them, or if they were just dreaming.

Looking up, they both see Paen squatting above them. Both notice his erect hardness displaying itself. His organ throbs, as they both rise, coming closer to investigate him now. Both want his undivided attention, seeing as how it was he that disturbed both of them, both wanting fulfilment that only he can provide. Avicia knows all his talents as well as what they both relish. He can light both their individual fires, first time, every time. Nefatia knows the missionary position, and now she wants to know more. Avicia told her there is so much more to learn. She will have to try everything to find what she enjoys most to discover her favourite. At least she has time on her side. Paen's persistent caresses, toying, reaps benefits. Showing a little white covering, across their radiant pinkness. Paen gets down, lapping away the cream from both pairs of thighs. Agitating, pushing his oral muscle in. past all four labia. Sweeter than warm milk from a cow. Slurping, eager not to miss a drop; he doesn't, as he drinks them both dry. His coarse tongue rasping across, over their love lips, their pubis, the vaginal crown and walls; both satisfied, pink cheeks, sparkling eyes.

Avicia is the first to respond. A full, wanton, wet kiss atop his raging, petulant, shiny dome.

"Good morning Avicia, good night's rest?"

"Yes Paen, you have had breakfast, now it is my turn.."

She takes hold of his burning organ, placing it in her mouth. She gobbles and twists him, setting him on fire. Making his erect shaft, excel. She feels him throb, erratically sliding his length in and out of her mouth, running her teeth along his pulsing vein and pushesthe tip of her tongue into the eye of his red crown.

"Come Paen, I want all your juices, thick and sticky now. I am hungry for you and only you. I know you are close to letting me have my way."

"I know I will give in eventually, ohhh, I can feel my juice, I know so. Can you, Avicia?"

She was rubbing hard, long, with short fierce strokes. Squeezing, she forced him to the back of her throat. His climax was vivid, extreme and powerful. She kept him locked in her mouth, drinking all of him. Finally subduing his and her own desires. Quelling his riot, but still amazed that he was till erect.

"Nefatia, come it is your turn, Paen is still hard, he wants you now!"

"Paen, that is very large and so thick!" Nefatia said, as she wrapped her hands around his manhood, feeling his body heat, twisting and twirling him, smiling into his eyes.

"Where would you like me?"

"Nefatia, you stay there, I will come to you. I am going to make love to your perfect, full, round breasts."

But first he parted her tight labia, licking them both gently, his tongue darting in between her tight, curly bush. He is looking, seeking for the pink, sweet, delicate morsel below hidden amongst her pubic flurry. Feeling her wriggle and gyrate, he knew he had found her little button. So he licks her spot softly, making her love lips curl back. Gaining entry into her with the point of his tongue. Ensuing deeper, ever deeper into her bodily delights, her sultry, scented snatch. Making her honeypot boil, with all his immediate attentions. Tasting her divine sweetness across his coarse, lavish tongue, not a drop of her precious love juice was spilt.

Then he sat up and mounted this glorious, vivacious woman. His hardness was more visible, pronounced as he slides it in between the bosom of Nefatia.

"I hope you are going to enjoy this, goddess. Can you feel my erection, how gently it throbs?"

"Yes Paen, I can feel you. I can see you as well, so well developed. Your shiny crown is pointing its eye at me."

Paen then wraps both of Nefatia's soft, warm orbs over his quaking, stiff organ. Then with a gentle rocking motion, sliding, slipping in between her two mounds of flesh, he gets very excited. She pushes her tongue out, to see if she could reach his erect, glowing staff and lick him as he in turn arouses her with his tingling, rampant rod. But now she knew she wanted him somewhere else, her body itching for his flesh, "Paen, you put my body in turmoil. I want you inside me, please."

"As you wish Nefatia. I will get off you. Then I want you to turn over, so you are on all fours."

As he gets off her turns and goes up on all fours, she offers herself to him.

Paen feeds his swollen and excessive pole into her dark, foreboding body, the most gorgeous, erotic flower he had ever seen. That dark, auburn hair has falling across her shoulders. Her big, absorbing, brown eyes look through him into his very soul. They know who he was, what he was, but saying nothing.

"Come Paen, I want all your juices, thick, sticky inside of me. So help me, I want your hard, round, long staff, delivering all your love to me. In one thick, sticky stream!"

"OK my diligent, delightful lady, anything you demand will be yours." In his excitement he transmutes in to in werewolf form.

So he pushes headlong into her joyful tightness. He twists, turns, his slow deep strokes penetrate as she takes all of him, up to his hilt. holding himself there. She can feel the pressure mounting within; his bevelled dome sticky, the eye expanding. Withdrawing, he clashes against her nubile, resilient thighs; he pushes forward grunting, she lifts herself to meet all of his surge. Nefatia wet and soaking, sticky. Both pairs of loins and thighs are covered in the ladies' excess. Paen lurches uncontrollably they both defy gravity, for a second! Then crash back down to her bed. Paen having exploded with his cum, fills his lover to the very brim, to overflowing. Enriching both their hot, eager bodies, as well as caking the both of them in his excess lava. Both felt filled with pleasure, so happy neither noticed the aftermath of their involved lovemaking. Just enjoying the consummation of their carnal pleasure. Wanting it to last for as long as possible. Neither of them moved an inch, for a considerable amount of time.

Once he had relinquished the beauty that was Nefatia, he sat between them both, looking at them. Long, lost in their never ending eroticism, pleasure and womanly magnificence. Both as fragrant as the wild briar. Both evenly matched with their outstanding beauty; Nefatia and Avicia, both with the heavenly tone, the hue of the colour of midnight. This is what made them both so spectacular. Paen reverting back to his human form.

"Paen, that was magic, every nerve in my body was alive and tingling. I do have so much more to learn from you. Please teach me all that you know. Avicia, I need to learn from you too."

"Nefatia it will be my pleasure to teach you, how to enjoy, I am sure Avicia will show you all that she knows as well. But I need to tell you both about my patrol I did earlier."

"What did you discover."

"Well Avicia, something similar to the other day. I was tramping around when I came across a large pauper's grave. It was not closed off, but still open. I stood back for a while, then silently three bodies attempted to climb out. I moved in, to put a stop to their misadventure. I spoiled the three, by ripping their throats out. Then instead of carrying on, they just fell back into the burial hole, lifeless, just like they should be. So I now know that if the bodies are disabled or incomplete, they cannot perform the task, the purpose they were bought back to life for. So we have to treat them all the same just make sure they are not living first. After that, just make sure they are incomplete, unable to perform any sort of function."

"Let Nefatia and myself get dressed, then we will come out with you."

The two women rise, Madonnas both of them, immaculate. Both sinners no doubt! But that makes them so much more desirable, wanton, doesn't it?

He stands there watching them both get out of bed, they both make him rise. He gets a touch of the wandering hands. He cups Avicia's amazing breasts, kissing her nipples longingly. She smiles as her hand, taking hold of my pulsing shaft, squeezing him boldly, pulling him softly and wistfully. Then Nefatia comes over, turning he sucks on both of her magnificent orbs. He then runs his tongue around both of her uneven large aureoles. He runs his fingers through her tight, curly bush just as she plays with his hard, thick and very aroused manhood. But she cannot help herself as she pulls her hand making him swell even more. She looks at him as he swells, watching his dome turn from red to scarlet. Then suddenly she has her mouth over him, sucking and drinking him, tormenting and sucking the very life from him. As his swelling lingers he stands back, finally letting them both get dressed, ready for the day's excursion.

We decide to split up, Paen alone, then Nefatia and Avicia team up, feeling safer together. They leave by the main gate, Paen leaping the wall and landing on four padded paws; sleek, silver, silent always in the shadows. Always looking for infamy. He keeps away from open areas, out of sight, skulking in the denser scrub. He is trying to figure out who is imposing their will on those that have passed on, into the afterworld. Who would be strong enough to arouse to awaken the dead. Then to be able to put them to some personal use, outside of any normal realm of activity regardless of the outcome. Some exorbitant overriding apocalypse. Just to help, assist to some little personal gain.

The archdeacon revelling in his new armour. His resources are a little slow in coming to his beck and call. Feeling a little self-assured that the more he used the power, the easier it is going to become. He felt the power of five revived. A surge forced itself through his mortality, his physical being. It felt like a new beginning. Four new life forces entered his lone, single portal. All their thoughts, memories, desires, invading, charging through in no specific order; churning, rattling, being absorbed; disengaging all his own personal thought process. He sits in a quandary, adjusting his will, backtracking, squeezing his desire, his dream back in amongst all the mental paraphernalia now occupying his ever-expanding brain.

The priest now more alert than he was ever before. He feels the archdeacon burn within him. Everything before this moment is lost, gone, vanquished. The dean, a kind and generous young man, now belongs to the archdeacon. A piece of his inner being craves for what is his, or was his. Now so much closer. Now he has the blackness consuming him; the sexton at a loss as to what exactly happened in that moment. He cannot remember what day it is or what was his last action or idea. He dismissed it as himself just being a little forgetful, due to his age.

The archdeacon implanted that readily available thought to save any confrontation. Also, finally savouring the Bishop John Gynwell's thoughts, deeds, misdeeds, misadventures. His personal unholy mess, now held within the fortress, that is the archdeacon, John de Offord.

The Bishop awakens. Smiling so sure now. He unlocks the connecting door, naked upholding his glaring hardness. He approaches the nubile Amora as she sits up, eyes wide open,

"My delicious young girl, I have this for you. He is splendid and awaits your attention."

She loves the hardness and the raging throbs. But she has always enjoyed the Bishop, the only man she has ever known up to now. She gleefully runs through to his bed. He climbs up and slips so nicely into Amora's soft, silky thighs and into her slightly quivering quim, deep and fully overloading her sensual delights.

The archdeacon could feel every stroke, touch and caress. He even felt himself get thoroughly aroused for the first time ever. Now back in complete control, furtively, fully disposed, of all four extra energies at his disposal

Nefatia and Avicia are out on the prowl together. Safe and secure; hand in hand with a new adventure. But how big an adventure was it going to be? They keep to the main highway, not wanting to get jumped by anyone as they stroll, not seeing anything out of place. The common populace is vanishing quicker than they can reproduce. A long day indeed. The sparsely populated villages, hamlets and, single building farms, all as they should be.

The evening lingers just a little. The moon is larger now, as if bolstered by the starlight. There was a twinkling and shining to guide Avicia and the goddess as they fade into the voids, where the hidden corners are waiting for the unexplained to reveal itself.

Sitting covertly, silently waiting for the mischief to fracture, display itself, reality to kick in. The reincarnated to be summoned, from somewhere. Unabashed, they sit close together to keep warm by sharing each other's body heat. Then a shuffle, a slight noise; after searching all day, a forlorn, deplorable body appears from the depths of the gloom. Nefatia jumps out in front of it – yet there is no reaction; no jump, no confrontation. Just a forward motion, heading somewhere, to who knows where!

Avicia steps forward, her fingers pressed lightly on her forehead as Nefatia holds the body still.

"She is heading towards a small, local church. She has been summoned by someone whose true identity is rather obscured. I can sense the source is not completely at the church, but that is the starting point for us."

"Avicia, should we just let her go, follow and see what besets us at this holy place?"

"I think that will be the wisest solution, Nefatia. Otherwise we will make no inroads to this reoccurring problem."

"Then my mystic siblys, that is our plan: to find the spirit that devises this dark sorcery."

They kiss the long, gentle kiss of sisters, of bondship of new lovers. They release the scabrous body, letting it lead them through the night to its evidence resting place.

The werewolf had no other plan than to leave anguished, disfigured corpses in his wake. It kills the already dead but leaves the physical evidence well out of sight. He was beginning to realize this was no mass orgy of rising bodies. Rather it is a pulling together of some form of kindred spirits required for someone's rather obtuse reasoning. For if someone had the power to recall the dead, then why just choose such a small number? All the same a rather macabre way of dealing with whatever situation, which was galling the said spirit.

With this idea settled within himself, why not just follow a body to see what type of sepulchre or mausoleum they lead him to.

As the night gets darker his pure, brilliant, amber eyes perceive the light that is readily available. He is able to follow the single body at a distance, without being seen. Without distracting, the sense or senses, of the thing in front of him. But he is wary, careful, as the trek seems to be coming to an end.

His sensitive nose is attracted to two new scents. He smiles within himself as recognition of the delicate scents tells him who they both are. Coming from behind, he stalks them both, staying in his werewolf form. Making contact with his two compatriots, he licks them both with his coarse, rapturous tongue, giving them both a start. They both turn to him, stroking him, enjoying the feel of his fine, velvety, silver coat, “Is that you Paen? So perfect.”

“You were so quiet I did not hear you approach. Even your low breathing, did not give you away.”

Sitting in between them, “Yes, I followed one of our bodies to this little church. I wonder why this one in particular?”

Avicia says, unable to take her eyes off the werewolf, watching him speak, “How about if we can find a way in, to see if we can find the priest within.”

Nefatia adds, “Then our clever young seer may be able to get some information, from him.”

“Wait for me here. I will go and determine the best way in, then come back and get the both of you.”

Bounding away, gone before they can reply into the chilly, unwelcoming night. The two women cuddle and snuggle up close together to keep out the damp, cold night air.

The werewolf returns, smothering the two beauties with his inexhaustible body heat. His coat gives them back their lost warmth. Once they could both feel their limbs, they struggled to get up; increasing his size, standing still for them, he allows Nefatia and Avicia, to mount him, to ride him. Both hugging, clinging to his long, shaggy, silken coat as within the blink of an eye, he starts, stops; outside a small dwelling, right at the back of the church. They watch as the priest is in the process of putting on his regalia. Then he walks into the silence of the mother church.

The trio creep into the vestry, looking out into the womb of the church, wonderment across all their faces.

The congregation at this early hour, long before sunrise, amounts to no more than twenty bodies. The priest holds out his arms, casting them over the conventicle, saying thus,

*Rashpaya colligate*
*hi errant,*
*perdidit animarum*
*in diligendi net.*
*Facere aliud quidem*
*pro his desecration*
*ecclesie nostre and*
*filias Eorums.*

Having stated his small personal chant, which was sounding like a prayer to the Almighty for gathered congregation.

Nefatia and Paen both looked at Avicia, she eyed them both;

"His chant went something like,
Kashpaya Gather
these wayward
lost souls,
into our loving net.
To make the one
pay for his
desecration of our
church and
their daughters."

The very small patronage of this assembly stayed in their seats. The priest vacated his pulpit and returned to his vestry. There he sat intense, alone like a font as something bubbled just below the surface in complete control. He jumped out of his lethargy, his self-sustained dream, as the three seemed to approach him, appearing from nowhere.

"Welcome to the house of God. His love is yours today."

"Thank you, Father," Avicia said as she took hold of his proffered hand, making the physical contact that was needed to engage her abilities as a sibyls, her physic ponderings. Casting her mind deep within his self. Unable to see or touch beyond but could see a face; lingering, not for long.

Then the connection is broken.

The goddess unrestrained, unrivalled, flexes her muscles. Her smile is gone. Without a second thought she draws her falchion, whistling through the air, cutting through his breastplate without slowing her speed and dexterity. She splits the priest clean in half. While the heart is still warm, beating its last as the blood still flows around it Nefatia lunges in, devouring the pumping muscle of the dead priest. Within two massive bites it is vanquished, gone! She stands hands aloft, her sword raised to the heavens. Her beautiful face is smattered with fresh, congealing blood. Her eyes, pupils, iris, retina are all crimson. Snorting her cry deep from her lungs, she fills the air as it echoes, echoes, reverberates and resounds. Her hair is on fire like a scarlet flame, red and burning angry flames aloft. The symbol of the Sisterhood! Recharging her desire to follow in her mother's footsteps. Reclaiming her right, as the first daughter, alongside her first kill. Her hair flowed all the way down to the small of her back. Flaring, on fire, no danger to her; as she grew in stature, to a great physical height. Looking every inch the Goddess, all in black.

Once the surge runs the course of her wild, virile body, she degenerates back into the powerful young woman she was to start with.

The werewolf bounds into the church, reconciling the congregation back into the arms of their maker. Leaving the bodies, where they lay. Then back into the vestry, "Well my beautiful young women, what do you think our next positive move should be?

"Well Paen, I did see a face. That is all I have to go on. But one face amongst so many. But we must find him. It was definitely a man's."

"Paen, Avicia, as we find this person, or persons, I feel we must destroy the entity. One, so their souls will rest properly, for this eternity with whatever their god or creator may be. Also, the already dead must be laid to rest once again, so as not to upset the land of the living. "

"The perpetrator must be accountable. He, or they must pay for the upheaval and indiscretion, or their greed and irreverence to life itself," Avicia added

Nefatia went on, "That is why I killed the priest. If need be, we will purge ourselves and the whole community of them, one at a time."

"I agree with both of your sentiments. But I think we need to go back to Riche Mont. For the horse, along with his cart, this could involve a lot of travelling. So we will need to make ourselves as comfortable as possible. Or you make yourselves comfortable here. I'll go and fetch the cart, then bring it back to you, here. Then we start our trek."

They both reply together, "We all go together, back to the homestead. Get everything we need, then start the hunt as one unified party. We'll all be in it together, until the final outcome. The Sisterhood unites us, just as Mother does."

"OK, then we can all rest here. When the sun rises, we make our way back to Riche Mont, our lair."

Paen becomes the silent shadow as the two women lay their heads, asleep in an instant. It reminds him of the many times he did the selfsame thing with his first mother, the she-wolf. Reminding him how safe, secure and warm he felt, snuggled deep into her fur. The sun rose all too soon, sharing its warmth with the trio. He whispered in their ears so very softly, they only just heard him.

As he transmuted, they sat astride his back. Still half asleep, they found it hard to come to their full awareness, to be wide awake. By the time he got to the entrance Nefatia was fully awake. Jumping down from his back, she cast the sign at the gate, whispering the magic syllable. The gates open as the three cross the boundary. Paen heads for the stables, hitching their favourite horse to the cart. He himself was ready to venture forth into the unknown. Availing himself of the large pantry, he makes food available for all. To eat now and enjoy before they sallied forth, into their personal conflict, either physical or mental. Not completely sure what they were getting one another into, but all willing to go forward, to see what lay ahead.

He was ready and eager to set off. The horse and cart at their disposal. Rations, vitals they had at their convenience, were packed, along with the horse feed he loaded.

Not wishing to squander time unnecessarily, he sauntered down to Avicia's room. Opening the door, he came across two naked bodies, threshing together. Squealing, giggling and touching they caressed first softly, then hard. He stood watching the two wanton beauties, enjoying the fine display of four breasts, along with their majestic nipples bobbing up and down. Limbs intertwined, crissing over one another as their red-hot lips smacked against each other, their finger through their hair. Digits penetrating loins, slipping into pubic-covered quims.

Paen got down behind Nefatia. His rod was exposed, erect, over-ripe; hot slipping himself from behind, into the goddess' tight buttocks. Such relief from her nubile, frantic torso. He licked her earlobes, nibbled and kissed her neck. Running his fingers across her glorious breastshe cupped and squeezed them. Toyin and tweaking, he squeezed her mighty nipples too. Caressing her uneven aureoles, his fingertips went around, around both of the darkened circles. He could feel her thighs squeeze, gratifying his thickness just as his aroused dome tickled her tender, round bottom. She wriggled uncontrollably, knowing who was behind her.

"I thought you were going to stand there all morning, just watching the two of us Paen."

"Your two bodies just hypnotized me, arousing me all the while."

"Paen, do not forget your promise, to show me how much more you can do to me. To increase the pleasure, I can get from you."

"Nefatia, I will show you all that I know. Are you enjoying me at this moment?"

"Yes, but press a little harder, I want to feel you, so much closer than you are already."

Paen pushes in closer to Nefatia, feeling himself penetrating her tight derriere, "Ooohhhhh, You naughty boy, so thick, so long, you throb continuously my dear."

"Yes, it is all for you, my goddess. But I think first, we need to sort out this blight of dead bodies. Who, why, someone would want to resurrect them."

Avicia responds, "I know, we just got carried away with our own self-interests."

Paen cups Nefatia's magnificent bosom, pulling himself deeper into her, she is desperate to mount him. He cannot help himself, losing all self-control as he ejaculates, gyrating within her clutches, unable to stop. Filling her, spraying himself wildly. It had been a while since touching her divine body, having complete satisfaction. He now has it all, in one glorious moment. Still hard, needing to satisfy himself; not liking himself, for just using these two young women, at this precise moment, for his own sexual relief. But he moves over to Avicia, and she takes hold of his erratic tool. He feels her coarse, curly bush graze his bulbous crown as she misaligns him, stubbing his opulent greedy crown against her Venus mound in her eagerness to have his staff inside her, as quickly as possible. Quickly he remedies this, taking his manhood in his hand and inserts it into her ravenous, very receptive body. Wanting him as deep as possible, all of him, sunk to grind her clit. She rides him hard, like the devil. She feels his cum almost immediately gorge into her, filling her, relieving her need for a man. He pumps his juice into Avicia, liking her warm torso as she threshes alongside of him.

Both women enjoy his participation. He assumes he satisfied both. He kisses both pairs of lips when proffered to his, long, hard and deliberate. As a lover, beau, sweetheart. Neither letting him go, four arms around his neck; both wanting, needing his complete, undivided attention.

"OK Avicia, Nefatia, I enjoy you both as much as we need each other. I always will. The pair of you, frolicking naked in front of me, was superb. With such complete abandon, you excited me, aroused me. I wanted you both. My sexual appetite as a werewolf takes me over sometimes. But we do have a job to do. I have made food for us all. You both get ready. I will load the cart with what you both need. We eat, then we leave."

"OK Paen, what are you taking?"

"Nefatia, I have all that I need with me now."

"Paen, are you sure?"

"Avicia, I am all that I need, at any time, I can assure you. I promised Mother that I would protect you, keep you safe from harm. That now includes Nefatia. I am my own weapon."

The three of them are now a lot happier that they are to go together, stay together, no matter what happens and no matter what comes their way. They all huddle close and eat and drink so very quietly.

Then, mounting the horse and cart, they start out on their adventure.

# CHAPTER THIRTEEN

John the archdeacon felt a sudden jolt! It was as though part of him had been ripped from his very being. He tried reclaiming him; but no response, no cry for help. No pang of regret, no soul-searching just a candle being put out. He had more resources to use, to acquire from his fearsome lord, but that would mean using his own name. A dread, that would cost him dear. So for now, he had three other cohorts at his disposal, to form a barrier to protect him. His wisdom, knowledge acute senses would tell him when his situation was dire. When it was close to him, forfeiting his purpose. When he have to feel that word, tumble from his very own lips; for his own physical salvation. But for now, he was safe.

The dean guided to a hideaway, safely out of sight. Only he knows where. To be able to cast his net of consciousness even wider than before. He has to fish for every last soul and make the blasphemer, fear for his life. But even more horrific, his very soul, along with his travels, would be affected also.

The sexton now offay, with his existence. His moments of self-doubt; his willingness to be led, by some ethereal supposition. Frustrated he got lost in his ways, led from the path of righteousness. But in the end, capitulation reigned supreme. Life rolled along as he continued his search for the names that eluded him. He had all the registers he needed, it was painstaking work. But he was told by a little voice within him that he could do it. So he believed with all certainty that he could achieve his goal. He believed in his own ability to succeed.

So the sexton, Thomas de Herdwick resumed with his research. Looking for as many of the dead relatives of all the young girls that had been used, seduced by the antics of Bishop John Gynwell. With the hope that the necromancers could bring them back to the realms of the living, to haunt and feed on the fear of the Bishop. In the hope that they would consume his essence and energy with a continual attack on his very soul. Then take him with them on their return to whatever eternal life may or may not exist after our mortal coil expires.

John Gynwell is subversively being used as one of the necromancer's acolytes along with the sexton, deacon and priest. He was too busy cavorting with Amora. She was with him night and day. She made him erect with her hot, delightful little digits. Then sucked him. Mounting his manhood, she just sat on him. She enjoyed his hardness, thickness, his body within hers. He enjoyed the pleasure of her tight pink muff, squeezing his rigidity. He played with her firm, perfectly formed breasts, pulling and tweaking those haughty nipples. He forgot all about his favourite, Malyna.

Malyna had found the time to disappear to the cathedral with a new young priest into one of the side altars. Defrocking the priest, she showed him how to love her with his young, fresh, virgin manhood. Such a lovely thing, untouched, unspoilt by anyone else, hers from the very beginning. Unlike her time with the Bishop, she was beneath him as he bucked and lunged, fully inserted, into his little piece of paradise. As they coupled on the altar the priest prayed for his fruits to be received, both to be satisfied. Then for forgiveness, for performing, these rites, for desecrating a sanctified altar. As the priest ejaculated within her little tabernacle, so did she. They both smiled at each other, saying, "Amen."

He stayed deep within her, luxuriating in her soft, furry quim. She lay on her back, happy for the first time that someone else had done all the work. She had just laid on her back, thoroughly enjoyed, been pleasured, with every stroke and every inch he had supplied. She could feel his juices squirting into her famished pussy with her dress, high up above her waist as the priest loomed naked above and on top of her, sweet body. They kissed, so many amorous pecks; he did not want to let her go.

"Take me back to your dwelling, then you do not have to let me go."

"Yes my delicious child, come with me. Help me dress, then we can go there."

Helping her down from the altar, he made sure her dress covered her modesty, along with everything else. Then using the shadows, hidden corners, recesses, while no one ever saw them; they sneak off to his abode to eat. Then share their love all over again. The Bishop is in a world apart, due to the powers and intervention of the archdeacon.

# CHAPTER FOURTEEN

Nefatia and Avicia are riding up on the horse and cart. The stealth of the werewolf out in the undergrowth, oblivious to his own safety and purely there to protect his two allies, his two favourites. They headed away from the safety, security of Riche Mont into the wild, unexplained interior of Rutland, England. Into a world of wonder and amazement and weird happenings daunting!

But unflinching, with only the safety of the trinity to protect all three of the adventurers. Their weapons only beholden to them. Paen his power, might, stealth, keen senses, self-preservation.

Avicia, her patience, foresight, her ability to see beyond into the paranormal. To see, feel through physical touch, the nuances invisible to others.

The goddess, Nefatia's, sword, Heartbreaker, is attuned only to her. Her knowledge of war and sheer presence and persistence, her ability to not shy away from anything, ever.

Paen surges naked as the day he was born, apart from the abundant, coarse hair carpeting his robust, heavy body.

The svelte, hypnotic Avicia is bathed in a scarlet, full-length, figure-hugging dress.

Then came the imposing figure of the goddess, squeezing into a sheer pink full-length silk gown. Her vivacious body clings to the attire rather than the dress draping her desirous, devilish torso.

Having made sure they were both safe, and having all kissed each other once again, then again, the horse and cart sets out on its journey. Paen fades into the background, nowhere to be seen. He was in fact beneath the cart, just near enough to rip out anyone's throat should they be silly enough, to try and attack the occupants. Not sensing any immediate danger or impending threats, he slopes off into the surrounding leas, meadows and copses. There is nothing to daunt him there either, so he brings back with him a brace of rabbits and hare. Throwing them into the back of the cart, ready for dinner later.

Then they make a short stop and break open a jug of mead. Each of them takes a healthy swig or two. This allows Avicia a chance to use her ability to see if she can register a direction, a hint of where they should be going. Maybe she can remember his face, if a name comes to mind or any small thing that did not seem important at the time, but would be important now, help them on their way. She knows there is something she is missing. It eludes her at this moment in time. But it will come to her. They move on once again, Paen the werewolf bounded ahead, looking for a secure camp site before the sun finally goes down.

An old run-down barn looks good. It is big enough to put the horse and cart in to its interior, as they do not want to draw any unheeded attention to their progress, if at all possible. A fire is soon started, the hares skinned, gutted and cooked over the open flame. The heat drew all three of them closer one another. Avica drew on her psychic reserve, casting her mind back to the priest. This time she recalled more than his face! But the dog collar, around his neck, with the reddish vestment, around which the collar sat. Avicia imparts the information to her two friends, "Paen, Nefatia? I think I have just remembered something. The face I saw, he was wearing a dog collar, with a red garment underneath."

"Avicia, that is good. But does it help us, in our quest?"

"Nefatia, it does, in a way. The dog collar obviously means the church is involved again. I think the red will determine his position, or rank, within the church. I know the normal priest just has a black cassock."

"That is good work. So we need to start at the church first, wherever we end up."

"Yes Paen, thank you. I need to approach the parish priest. Enquire about his station. It is only me who can give a full description of him. So it will be you and me, Nefatia. While Paen keeps his silent watch as usual."

They all agreed to Avicia's summary.

Having eaten their fill of spit roast hare, drank a little of their wine. With Paen in the middle she could snuggle close to him to gather in his bodily warmth. They all slept silently and peacefully through the night.

The neighing of the horses alerted him. He transforms himself as he leaps to attack the aggressors, all in one go. Pegging both miscreants down before they could take another step, he leaves both with their throats torn, ripped out. They are dead in an instant, not knowing what laid them to sleep. He carried both bodies out of sight into the darkest corner, where they would not be seen, ever.

Then he kept his peace, along with a silent watch through the rest of the night. Checking their provisions, he lit a fire for warmth. The meal was all ready when the two glorious maidens awoke. Unaware of the night's intrusion, they make ready eating as Paen fed the horse, then hitched him to the cart, dowsed the fire and lifted the two beauties onto the cart. In this way they continued their quiet journey. They were heading towards a small hamlet, of two or three houses, no church, so there was no stopping. The wind faded, the sun shone, pleasant and warming; the two women chatting quite happily. Paen skirted the dwelling as the horse and cart trundled across the main thoroughfare. They find no one about, it is a virtual ghost town. They carry right on passed the houses, through the fields, and past one or two farms. At last they pulled over into a sweetly scented meadow for the chance to taste the air, smell the wild flowers and listen to the songbirds. But they avoid the rats, as well as the fleas!

Only the voices of the three travellers could be heard. The wildness is supreme and enticing. Again Paen lift both women onto the cart.

Now they head out onto the open road. The horse just keeps rolling along at a nice steady pace, majestically trotting forward. In the distance they can see Hambleton, but they're not going to make it, before nightfall. So the werewolf goes out forward, looking for an empty barn or outhouse they can use for the night.

Perfect! The werewolf comes across some deserted stables. He races back, guiding the cart in. All is now nice and homely, warm for the night ahead. The pot is bubbling away nicely over the open fire. The horse has his nosebag. They break open a small bottle of wine, handing it around. Paen spoons out the meal onto their plates. Tucking in, they enjoy the close company and chat, as well as the remaining wine. He goes down into the stables proper to lay down some hay, thick enough to keep out the cold. Also he makes beds available on the back of the cart.

"I have prepared your beds on the back of the cart. I have made my bed on the stable floor. I will be up early in the morning. So you both get a good night's sleep, ready for tomorrow. When we venture into the town before us."

Nefatia and Avicia whisper, plotting, as they leave to retire for the night. Paen subdues the fire, to keep the warmth. He gets himself comfortable on his pile of hay. Laying back, he rests as it is early still. He contemplates what was likely to happen if they find the person they were chasing.

Hopefully it would happen, sooner rather than later. His attention is disturbed by female laughter - a few giggles, then silence.

Then the sound of unshod feet approaches him. He sat up, focused completely. Instantly attentive; his very personal companion, stiff, erect; a burning sensation in his eager loins. There before him stand the goddess and the psychic. Both are exquisitely naked, both wanton standing directly in front of him. Looking down at Paen; both gleaming, their two bodies shimmering in the moonlight. Both pairs of eyes are like scalding coals, eyeing him up and then down.

"Well ladies, do join me. I am all yours. Come, sit beside me, I can relieve the tension if you have any. If not, perhaps you would like to relieve my pent-up pressure!"

Together they come, sitting either side of the lone man. Their two hands gently rubbing, sooth and ease my cumbersome erection. One hand belongs to Nefatia, the other with eager digits to Avicia. Both are keen to get the knot out of his taut, thick muscle. It always feels good to be in the hands of a woman. Any woman can caress expertly, but it is so much more potent when it is two women. That doubles the joy, yielding the excruciating pleasure at the hands of these two maidens - slow, excessive long strokes. Then comes the licking and sucking of the two fierce, fiery tongues. They generate just enough power to relieve the latent, throbbing tension he holds within. The sudden, pent-up release is just overwhelming. Their lips and hands work in complete unison. Avicia moving to sit in front of Paen. My turn to enjoy, as he enters her tight tabernacle, with his flashing, rushed oral muscle. Making her push hard against him. He pushes and delves even deeper so he can taste all of her heaven on his lips. Nefatia makes sure he stays erect for her, stroking his rampant staff vigorously. Then not to be outdone, she sits astride of his torso. Her quivering pussy, flush, against his very willing, bevelled crimson dome. She pushes down swiftly, taking his thick, hungry pole deep, deeper into her very tight, snug muff. Her pubis is soft as it sweeps across his gonads, as she sits like a queen on a very comfortable, live throne. He now has paradise mounted upon his manhood. Where else should she be?

He rises and rises to Nefatia's continuous manipulation and agitation. Her sensuous vaginal walls break down all his resistance, all of his manhood and elevates it to breaking point. Alluring and refined, the goddess gently applies the pressure of her formidable groin. That does it for him. He just loses all self-control. She is so tantalizing his love juice just flows a hot, white and sticky mess pumping into her delightful, threshing body. He still has Avicia sat on his face. She cums all over him. Her hot cream seeps at first, then gently flows over his face and to either side of his mouth, down his neck. Then across his matted, hairy chest.

"That was amazing, fabulous both of you. Together you are out of this world. You are both totally irresistible, either together or alone."

"We enjoyed you as well, we always do. We are off to bed now, see you in the morning.

"I will be prowling around, so sleep and just ignore me."

The stealth and silence of the werewolf unnoticed as he lopes out to the exterior of the stables, keeping the immediate area safe. All was quiet and it stayed that way all through the remaining night. Again the fire was set, the mead opened ready to imbibe. The cabbage soup was simmering. Now watered, the horse's head was in his nosebag. When Paen is all set to hit the road once more, the two females gently awake from their long night's slumber. No time is wasted as breakfast is taken and Paen is back to escorting the cart as the two women head on into Hambleton. Making their way straight to the large church.

Avicia goes to the house, knocking awaiting a reply. A priest answers, smiling, "Good morning my dear, do come in."

"Thank you, father."

"So, how may I help you, young lady, at this hour of the day?"

"I am trying to find someone. I have a feeling he is to do with the church."

"I may be able to help. Do you have any information about him?"

"Yes Father. I know he has a dog collar, with red material bene- "

"Well child, that would probably mean he was a dean. Do you know what he looks like?"

"Yes Father. I can give you a description, if that would help you."

"It would indeed. I might know of him."

Avicia gives the priest a memory picture, after recalling his face from her memory bank.

"Yes, that is one of the new dean's. He's fairly young for that position, but there's not much of a choice at this moment in time."

"Would you know where I could find him, or of someone that could tell me?"

"Yes, the archdeacon sent him to Barnsdale, for further training. To make sure he was up to his early promotion."

"So Father, where is Barnsdale?"

"Just the other side of the valley. Also, I have just remembered the Dean's name. Adam de Crosseby."

"That is wonderful Father. Thank you so much for your invaluable help."

"May God bless you, my dear."

Leaving the priest Avicia returns to the cart with Nefatia and Paen.

"Well, I have a name, also where he is now. He is training as a dean. He is Adam de Crosseby, working in Barnsdale."

"Well we know where he is, where we need to go straight away."

"Yes Paen. The other side of Greentham Valley."

"How long a journey is that going to be?"

"Well Nefatia, if we have travel through the vale, with the cart, then a good two days, even three."

"That is going to be a long tour, a hindrance we could have done without."

"Yes Nefatia, but nothing is in our control."

"Nefatia, Avicia, if you both stay here and keep out of sight, I will go get him. Then bring him back here to you. A day at the most for me, if I travel alone!"

"That is a better idea, I will keep my sword at my side at all times."

"In that case, Nefatia, get your sword out now. Then I will leave, right away."

In a whisper the metaphysical werewolf is gone, vaporised into the the shadows. Exercising his dominance, over his physical extremes. Claiming his full, optimum vigour, power and strength, he grows to a size which Avicia and the goddess have never seen before. A wolf the size of a Suffolk punch has been released. Its easy strides and deafening howl make it a threat to anyone daring to get in his way.

The countryside flashes by in a blur, the signs showing the way, the distance of no consequence. The valley lies quiet and subdued, there is not a living person in sight. Thanks to the fatal intervention of the plague, the crops have been left to die. Channelling his energy; the valley passes quickly behind. Beyond him is an elderly gentleman, not far in front of him. He slows, changes, walks by.

"Good day sir, could you tell me where the church is in Barnsdale?"

"Yes, young man. It is this side of the valley, just before you actually enter Barnsdale."

"Thank you for your time."

Paen carries on walking to put distance between himself and the man. As his pace quickens, so does his shape, speed and visibility. A breeze, which his inner-self the wolf, finally arrives at the church door. Allowing himself in as Paen, he ventures down the main aisle, past all the empty pews. Seeing at the fronta priest at prayer, Paen sits patiently while he finishes.

"Amen."

"Excuse me Father, I hate to bother you. But could you tell me, where the dean is?"

"Well young man, he is no longer here. He has been moved on."

"Would you happen to know where?"

"Yes, to a small hamlet, North Luffenham."

"Where? Could you help me with directions?"

"Like I say, a small hamlet North Luffenham. You need to head towards to Kilthorpe. Then onto Broccoli Bottom. It is hidden away, in a small dell."

"I thank you for your time, Father. God bless."

"Thank you. May he give you, his blessing too."

As he leaves the church, again he transforms. Once again he is out of sight of everyone. He tries to extend every fibre of his extraordinary being, forcing it beyond even his known extremities, boundaries, tolerances. He can feel himself grow and extend beyond his own self-control. He has the sense to stop and regain the control as he needs to help his two friends. So he keeps himself to a size that does not impede his work. He sniffs ahead of him and wades into the twilight, able to see all with his bright amber eyes. Closer, closer to Barnsdale. He encroaches on the borders. Continuing at a hurtling gallop, he presses on to the field; without stopping, into the stables. Smelling the trouble there, rushing in. He finds Nefatia and Avicia trussed up. The cart is being pillaged by ruffians and miscreants. He could not blame them, times were hard, desperate beyond comprehension. People were turning to crime just to survive, because there was no other choice.

Regardless, he wanted no harm to befall Nefatia and Avicia. Keeping his form as a werewolf, he crawled and bared his fangs and flashed his angry, large amber eyes. He rushed over to his two wards, releasing them immediately.

"Are you both all right? Unharmed?"

He licked them both, his long, rough tongue soothing them, making them feel quite at home.

"Of course Paen. We were safe as part of the Sisterhood. Also we knew you were out there, sensing that we were in danger. Then come to our rescue." They said as one.

Paen back with them. Smiling along with Avicia and Nefatia.

"Adam de Crosseby no longer works at Barnsdale. He has been moved to a hamlet called North Luffenham.

"Who moved him there?" Avicia responded.

"The archdeacon apparently."

"How far away is that, how much extra added to our journey?" Nefatia added, with a look of disdain.

"It is towards Kilthorpe. Then onwards to Broccoli Bottom. Ladies, can I suggest we eat now, get a good night's rest? Then get a move on in the morning."

"Good idea, Paen," they both reply, smiling at each other as they say it. He gets out bread, beef and pork pottage as well as wine to quench their thirst. All of them bed down together, keeping warm yet with safety in numbers the irst thought on their minds.

The horse and cart carries all three members of the small party. The quest continuing to discover the meaning of these resurrections. Driving the horse on, they only stop when they were able to take the horse to drink and feed him at the same time. The quiet is extensive and bewildering. They never pass a soul for hours at a time. Finally, at the end of the valley, Paen calls a halt. They pull over into a deserted, overgrown field.

"Nefatia, Avicia let us get something to eat and drink. You both sort that out. I will feed and water the horse. Then I will check the cart to make sure there is no immediate repairs required."

"How about sleep as well?" Avicia shouts out, making sure she gets the rest she needs, even if the other two do not need as much.

"Yes, Avicia we can do that too."

So they eat around an open fire, the heat, warmth of which draws all three very close together. Then Paen sees to the horse, the most important member of the team. Once again he checks the lumbering cart and greases it with animal fat to make sure the four wheels turn a lot easier. An outhouse discovered there. The horse, cart, as well as the three humans are all housed there for the night. For a good long rest, as the travelling had not finished yet.

They all wake together. Again the silent shadow sets an idea, to the rest of the adventurers.

"My two beauties, I want to carry on travelling onwards to North Luffenham."

"You are going to North Luffenham, by yourself? Will you be safe?"

"Yes, on both counts, my astounding, venerable siblys."

"To confront the dean?"

"Yes my mighty goddess. You just keep our sister here safe until my return."

"That goes without saying, Paen. But do not harm the dean."

"That is not my intention. My intention is to bring him back here, to be questioned by our sister, Avicia, with her many talents."

"Then bring him back swiftly to us. Be fleet of foot, let nothing stop or delay you, Paen."

Without a backward glance, as he leaves their presence. He is gone! Through Kilthorpe, deep into Rutland he goes, into the dell beyond Broccoli Bottom. He sees first the signs, then the boundary marker for North Luffenham. Slowing he changes his form from wolf to man. He sees the church at the other end of the village. Walking through, he nods to the very few people he passes. Finally finding the church along with its entrance, he gains a quiet entry, finding a conventicle already taking place with a very silent audience.

He sits at the back, not noticed by the congregation, which amounts to eight people in attendance. The service finishes. No one moves, only the priest; he comes over to where Paen sits all alone.

"My son, how can we help?"

"I am looking for Adam de Crosseby, the dean."

"You are in luck, that is me. How can I help you?"

Paen renders him unconscious. Then realizing the others were still seated, he goes over to them. Seeing that they were some more of the mindless husks, followers of the same cult or movement he changes his form long enough to dispatch all eight, to rest an eternal rest. He moves the bodies outside and hides them away in an outhouse to delay anyone finding them for as long as possible.

Picking up the dean, Paen advances with his eyes wide open, alert, attentive. He shoulders the burden without a breath or pause in his forward momentum. He makes his way back to the cart without any delay so that the seer could quiz him, as soon as possible. Hopefully this would put an end to the accumulating number of bodies.

Hiding in the amongst the scrub, woodland, copses, forest. Deserting the main byways and highways, away from prying eyes. Then coming out of the shadows, the mist of time, only when he is safely within the bounds of the horse and cart, along the with the two beauties he calls his allies. He catches them at Kilthorpe. He jumps aboard the cart with the body of the dean. Setting him down, he is gone again, shortly to returning.

"Follow me, there is a large Dutch Barn where we can hide away. So you can quiz the dean."

Avicia takes the lead. With no one else in attendance, they marshal the horse and cart into the empty barn. Making themselves comfortable, they share a jug of ale, onion and egg pie. Paen recoups the body, sitting him up; Avicia plants her hands either side of his head. But she senses absolutely nothing, no thought process at all, exuding from Adam de Crosseby.

"We will have to wait for him to come to his senses. I cannot get anything at all." As Avicia looks across at her sister.

"So we wait for him to regain consciousness." Nefatia replies.

"Nefatia, what other option do we have?" Avicia looks unable to hide her impatience.

Like a will o' wisp Paen has gone to the small brook he noticed earlier. Filling the bucket with the dirty, ice-cold water from the flow he returns and, without hesitation, throws the whole bucket over the oblivious dean. Shaking himself, Adam de Crosseby is roused, aware, conscious.

The syblis is motivated. Straight in with her delicate hands, she connects to his subconscious and reads as deeply as she can, feeling for anything, held within the mind of Adam de Crosseby.

She feels she sees another mind imposing upon his will. A glimpse follows a fleeting portrait of another face. Memorising that picture, she cannot delve deeper. She is fighting a force far stronger than her will. But she questions him directly, penetrating his mind alone. He only knows a little. The rising bodies are to do with someone's personal sexual gratification. The person causing the resurrection of these bodies has a personal vendetta against the perpetrator. Waiting to seek his downfall. Because of his corruptive, destructive influences. He wants the bodies to make reparation on the wanton depravity, destruction of these young lives who were all related in some way or another.

"Well I have another face, but no name. We do not know where he lives. He is tied in with the dean, along with the priest. It has something to do with unfriendly rivalry."

"Adam de Crosseby. Do you know who this man is? The one that sits beside you here, in your mind?"

"Madam, I do not know for sure. It was the archdeacon at Lincoln that sent me here. So he may be at the cathedral."

"Then may God save your soul, Adam de Crosseby."

The goddess stood above him and heartbreaker sang his death knell as he comes down with a vengeance upon him. Splitting open his chest it reveals the blood, gore and the smell of death as Nefatia once again claims a victim as hers alone. Planting her face in his chest cavity she gobbles at his very heart. With three vicious incisions her whole face is smothered in his blood. Her qui being released once again. Her long flowing hair ignited, into the many various tones, colours and hues of an open fire. The tongues of flame form an arch, around her head. Her wild eyes emit a forgotten anger as they shine red, as they bleed on their own account. She grows once again, infuriated by the meat and hot blood ingested into her. Nefatia's prowess is being rekindled, her perceptions redefined. Her guttural cry resounds far across the open leas, petrifying all that are within her audio range. That one cry defies retribution! A cry that defies everything else that cares to listen or dare reply.

# CHAPTER FIFTEEN

At exactly the same time Nefatia slaughtered the dean, the archdeacon felt the loss of another defence mechanism between him and his final goal.

He still had the protection of the sexton, his excellency Bishop John de Offord. But would that be enough as a cover, as a front for his final destiny? He would have to consider his options. Whoever was trailing him, was making very slow progress. But by killing his acolytes, they were going to find him eventually. He even felt the slow gradual loss of the dead that he was bringing back to the land of the living, to do his bidding and to confront the Bishop.

If one more of his shields or acolytes were discovered or destroyed, he would have to make the ultimate sacrifice for his final goal. In the crypt he had the incantation ready. But he would keep the sexton, as well as the Bishop, close by for his protection as well as using them to root out his enemies, his aggressors. Then discovering who they were, he would eliminate them; then get on with his life.

The sexton felt the jolt as well. It felt as if part of his family had just passed away. Someone familiar, no longer in the world of the living. But he could not stop or ponder, there was still work to do.

The Bishop had completed his letter to archbishop John de Stratford, who was travelling on a visitation in and around Canterbury and Ashford, regarding his thoughts on a visit from the present Pontiff. Bishop Gynwell had just delivered a High Mass alone, to a very receptive congregation in the Cathedral. He now sat down to lunch with his two admirers, Amora and Malyna.

"We enjoyed you performing Mass, Bishop John. It is always special, when the Bishop is there in person."

"Thank you very much Amora. Let me say grace, then we can eat."

Just as John finishes grace he feels the mind, the entity that is Adam de Crosseby go; as it is extinguished, obliterated, no longer part of his very being. But he feels his resolve is heightened, extended by a sudden surge of will power. Like a life force, some external presence bolsters his willingness to carry on. They eat in silence. But when they are finished, having consumed the last of the wine, they stroll, all hand in hand into Amora's bedchamber.

The scents and fragrances of a young woman linger in the very air, you breathe. Without assistance the Bishop disrobes. Malyna undresses the young Amora, but then excuses herself from the company. The Bishop and Amora touch, then kiss each other's body with passion and uncontrollable desire.The Bishop sucks those fine young pink nipples, pulling them with his teeth. Amora strokes that fine, fat staff, making it hard and thick just for her. Amora gyrates as John kisses her taut, firm breasts, caressing and then squeezing her nipples between his thumb and forefinger. He now gets up behind Amora and, pushing, rams his erect, rotund rod in between her tight, round, nubile buttocks.

"My that feels good, Amora. Just squeeze me harder. Bliss, my dear!"

Then he pulls out. Going round to her front he puts a cushion beneath her, lifting her midriff up before making sure he is still erect. In one wild swoop he gains the comfort of her loins. She parts her limbs as John the bishop successfully penetrates the delights of the young Amora. Enjoying his closeness, he enjoys her vivid tightness, which he was beginning to loose with Malyna.

Malyna goes through to her to her room then disappearing down the back stairs. She meets her new young priest. They sneak into one of the small chambers, off the main hall that no-one uses. The priest and his cohort walk through to the empty bedchamber. Kissing, kissing – there is so much kissing between the two of them. Enthralled with her newfound amour, he with his gorgeous young lady. She excites him, as it is she that permeates his naughty dreams, that makes him so wet.

She removes her dress, that is all she has on. The priest tackles his own garments. Immediately he is on his knees, sucking her hard, licking her tight bushy quim. Already he is hard and erect, extended and throbbing trying to learn self-control. Her hips are quaking, quivering, wanting that new bone inside her soon to arouse her, to make her wet. To ease the pain of losing the Bishop, to Amora.

But this one was good. By the time she had finished with him, he would be perfect for her. Feeling him go in was such a delight. As he pushed deeper, paradise was so close. He started pumping with such conviction, he made her wet – yet there was no climax. She clung onto his balls; then she rode him, wanting her satisfaction first. This she got in floods all over him. Now she removed her clamp like hands from his sac, the release urging him on for a little longer. Then he had his way, ejaculating into her already sticky quim. At last both were satisfied, and at least he was getting better. The very first time she had him, he was premature!

The archdeacon had no weakness or time to dream. His seething rancour driving him towards his only passion and desire. He has thought of everything. So these interlopers must be stopped. No more advantages are to be given to them.

# CHAPTER SIXTEEN

"Now tell me Avicia, how are we going to find our next link in the chain? We have no clues whatsoever." Nefatia asks her dear friend Avicia.

"Well Nafetia, what I suggest is we travel to areas of larger populations." Avicia replies.

"Why is that then, glorious syblis?" Paen cuts in and waits for a reply.

"Well, when you were bringing the dean back with you, I was concentrating on you, trying to see you. To follow your journey I forced my mind to expand, because I know of your two existences. So now I can follow you, but with the added bonus of seeing your other self." Avicia tells him.

"That is superb Avicia. So you can track me, as long as you focus on me in either form?" Paen smiles back happily.

"Yes, I also knew you had someone with you. At one stage I managed to see his face. It was then I knew you had our man. I told Nefatia that you were on your way here. That is why we were both ready for you, when you arrived with the dean in tow." Avicia tells them both.

"Paen, she is right. She did tell me you had de Crosseby with you. So she can match faces, if she sees the right face." Nefatia adds to the conversation.

"So we can also ask at churches like we did last time. Avicia can give the description. People do talk to women more readily than men, quite happily." Paen adds without any argument from the other two.

"Then that should be our plan, until we find them, Paen, Nefatia." Avicia is happier now they have a plan.

"In that case ladies, let's make something to eat. Bed down, then head out first thing in the morning. We have to try and cure this outbreak of obscenities somehow." Paen concludes.

They eat the rest of the egg and onion pie and helped down a small jug of mead. Clustering together by the cart, they drift off to sleep in a very untidy bundle.

Dawn was just breaking when Paen came to. Rising he took the horse to the stream to drink. Then giving him his nosebag, he lets him eat in peace. At the same time Paen checks his shoes, hooves and legs for any problems. Finding nothing, he finds little more wrong with the cart, just some re-greasing of the wheels with some spare animal fat, for smoother running.

He breaks out some bread to go with the three bolsters of pottage and a jug of ale. When all is in place and ready for the two women to state their hunger and thirst, the trio sit side by side with Paen in the middle; eating drinking their fill, they satisfying their bodily needs. Again fit and ready for travels, they head out along the main bridle path, out into the unkempt, barren land before them still infested with rats, fleas, dying livestock. Fields of dead cereal crops, neglected orchards and vegetable plots pass by as they forge onwards to try and upset this sect of blasphemers and depraved souls, trying to bring back the dead.

Anything they saw along the way that they thought could assist them in any way they picked up, scavenging anything useful to put in the back of the cart. They passed few people on their lonely journey for everywhere was sombre, deathly quiet and quite morbid.

The silent predator kept out of sight as he sallies forth making sure the way was clear with nothing to impede their progress. He collared a couple of vagabonds, struck them out without a moment's hesitation and dumped their ruined bodies well out of sight. On returning to the cart, he found the goddess standing over an impotent body of some unfortunate vagrant. Just taking his heart and eating it raw in its bloody state, feeling the satisfaction as his life force surged through her. Just accepting his life force into hers. Carrying on until just before nightfall, they come across a village.

The church is the first building they arrive at. Stopping, Avicia steps down and knocks gently on the door. A priest appears, unfazed by her appearance at this late hour.

"Good evening my daughter. How can I be of service to you?"

"Father, we are looking for someone. We were wondering if you might be able to help us, in any way."

"I can try my child. Can you describe him?"

"Yes, I can very vividly."

Avicia gives a detailed account of his face. She tells the priest she thinks he works for the church simply because those before have done. They included a priest, while the other was a Dean.

"I am very sorry young lady; I am unable to assist you with that. But I can offer you and your compatriots food, as well as somewhere to lay your head for the night."

"That would be very kind of you, Father."

"If you unhitch your horse, there is a modest stable just there. With a trough, oats, along with bedding."

"Nefatia, Avicia, you both go with the priest. I will sort out the horse and cart. Then I will join you all very shortly."

The priest guides the two ladies in, sits them down and says grace, then both join him in his supper. Paen takes a prowl before bedding down the horse. He then joined the merry throng at the table, chatting of happier times before the rise of the blight of the plague, the demise of most of the local farms. The priest shares his wine very liberally and they all enjoy one another's company. As the supper ends, it is quite late. The priest takes upon himself to show them to the spare rooms that he has. Avicia and Nefatia taking one, Paen takes the other. The priest gives them all his blessing and, since they are all tired from a very long day, they all soon fall fast asleep. The moment their heads hit the pillow, in fact. Except Paen, who takes one last stroll around the church. He also broke his sleep twice during the course of the night, just to make sure everything secure and to ensure there were no rapscallions about.

The priest did not seem put out by the fact, on the night before, by the lack of clothes on Paen's body. He did not object, in the morning; when he awoke everyone for breakfast, Paen was dressed in the very same way, once again. Avicia was dressed in a blue cotton frock and white chemise. Nefatia was adorned in an all-in-one pink linen full-length dress. Both very eye catching! It was a swift meal, after which they said their thanks to the cheery priest and asking him which way to go to more densely populated areas. He told us to head north-east, pointing the way ahead for us. As Paen put the two women up onto the cart. He himself jumping on the back; until he was out of the priest's view. Then he was back to running the verges, the scrub, the leas and the meadows; listening for, looking and seeking for the dangerous, the hidden, the chancer, the highway thief. As yet there was none, but they were just about to traverse a forest.

"Nefatia, keep Heartbreaker at the ready. I will be very close by. Avicia, focus for us. The horse will do what he does best - pull the cart, getting us through here safely in one piece."

The sun reaches its highest point of the day with the heat haze playing tricks, but Paen's amber eyes assured of no mirages or optical illusions. Yet he had no sense of foreboding and he was hoping to taste the air. Then above him in the trees he shouts a warning to Nefatia and Avicia. "Careful, they are lodged in the trees. Stay there just in case they try to net us. Just be patient and hold back."

Nefatia draws her falchion and as she anticipates the threat Paen shouts, "I am to the right of you and I'm ready for their mischief making."

So with the guidance from Avicia, the horse stands its ground. The ebony syblis keeps a tight grip on the reins, focussing into the canopy above them.

"I can see six idle bodies up there. Thinking they outwitted us. But be patient, because they are losing their patience altogether. They are just about to jump out of their cover, now!"

All six bodies land in unison brandishing their puny, archaic weapons. By the time Paen has disembowelled and dismissed four of them, heartbreaker has tasted blood twice, severing both ribcages so his mistress could taste the same blood as her sweet sword. As well as devour, ravage the brace of hearts, that were deservedly hers, hers alone. The trio was preserved and revered once again. Their bond gains strength, depth and fortitude. The rest of the journey through the forest was uneventful, very quiet; a solace in its very silence.

They found wild fruits, berries and various mushroom and other fungi to bolster their rather inadequate larder. The silence of the werewolf enables him fair game claimed a few rabbits, quail and grouse to share, along the way.

They came across the next farmstead just the other side of the forest. A dejected-looking woman, along with her malnourished baby daughter were sitting there.

"Good day mistress, what ails you on this fine afternoon?"

"Good day to you all. I despair of my luck. My husband was taken by the plague only a short day ago. So here I am with a new baby and no labour to assist me, and now my plough is in disrepair."

"Good lady, be of good cheer. Let us be your good fortune, let us be your Lady Luck. Tell us where to park our cart. I will repair your plough. Tell me of any other work I can do for you."

"I cannot thank you enough. Come in, come in. Eat with me first. Do you need clothes, kind sir? I have my husband's few clothes, if they would fit you or be of any use."

"Thank you for your kind offer, but I have always lived this way. Come, let us help you."

Paen helps the two women down from the cart. Bringing a little colour into the other's life. Never had she seen such material. The wealth of tones, sheens. The array and spectacle, beyond her wildest dreams. It blinded her senses.

"Ladies, may I touch your material? It is so magical, from a far-flung place. Come, eat with me, before it gets cold."

They all sat, partaking of the parsnip, turnip and onion soup. With the maslin, her fine cheese. Having had his fill of food, he stood up smiling,

"You ladies pray continue. I will go and do the repairs. I will return soon."

Paen went out. First he attended to the plough, finding one of the dowel pegs needed a swift repair along with the plough blades sharpening. They were minor jobs and did not take long at all. He went to check on her horse, where there was a problem there; his hooves needed cutting, along with new shoes, as well as fitting them. He went out to the cart, picking out his jute bag with his smithy tools held within. He found the woman's shed and, transforming into his other self, the werewolf he used his power, speed and dexterity to get the coals going. He brought her horse inside. Clipping and shearing the overgrown nails of the horse, he removed the old shoes along with the nails. Checking the size, he found the four that were nearest. Using the fire, he reshaping all of them to the correct size, as only a master smith could. Sshhing the horse to calm his fears of a rather strange handler, he fitted the shoes and nailed them on.

The horse runs away into the field, meadow grass at his hoofs. Part of her arable crop could yet be saved. Taking their horse, he hitches him to an open wagon and goes around collecting and harvesting what he can for the unfortunate woman. Then, using her fairly new thresher, he seperates the chaff from the wheat that she could now grind. From two small orchards of apples, pears and damsons he picks the ripe fruit for her. Finally, he decided that it would be good time to test the plough. To make sure his repairs could stand the physical trials, he hitched it to his body. Running as free as the wind, perhaps a little faster; he found he could make perfect furrows. Cutting all the tired, dead stalks and cereal head back into the earth, everything seemed to look so much better. The farm resembled a working farm once again. The harvest had been collected, the horse re-shoed, the plough repaired and the fruit in the barn was to be made into jams, preserves, pickles and chutneys. Her income would extend for a little while longer, at least.

He transformed just in time, as the three genteel ladies decided to appear.

"Goodness, what have you done?"

"Mistress, just a few repairs. A little harvesting, I had to check the plough worked, after my minor adjustments."

"That is just wonderful. Come in now, rest. I will cook, we can eat. You must stay the night. Then continue your travels in the morning."

"That is very kind of you, are you sure we are not putting you out?"

"Yes of course. I cannot repay you and your services, in any other fashion."

They all went in. Paen freshened up, then joined them all. The mistress of the house put ale, mead and small beer on the table along with beef and pork pottage, cabbage soup, cheese, apple tostee and fresh bread. It was a meal to delight everyone, especially as the lady of the house had not experienced company, at her farm, for the past seven months or more.

She only had one spare room. But they all assured her that would be adequate for their needs, it was causing no problem whatsoever. She went to see her baby.

The goddess and seer divested themselves of their clothes. Paen attached himself to the back of Nefatia. Kissing the back of her neck and running his fingers through her amazing, long thick hair, the colour of midnight. Tantalizingly rubbing her ears and lobes. Running a single finger over her eyes and down the bridge of her nose. Across her warm lips, as she nibbled his finger. Continuing down her fine, long neck, throat. Through the valley of her astounding breasts, where he cupped each beauty in both of his hands. She had felt him get harder, then harder and longer, thicker, the more he played with her. She was enjoying feeling his excitement, his instant appraisal of her glorious, nubile torso.

He was rubbing himself up against her continuously now. It was arousing her as well; she parted her warm and robust thighs to let him in, there to engage her hot delights and charms. She felt his hot bevelled, glossy dome against her tight little portal. Softly he pushed, parting the cheeks of her gorgeous, round, firm bottom. She sighed as his thickness engaged her willingly. Then his shaft fully penetrated, all the way in. She could feel his legs against hers, striving to get deeper. He caressed her full, round, firm bosom. Squeezing her thick, rampant nipples they squirmed in sheer delight, together as one. Gently slipping out of the goddess's tight grip, he whispers, "I am not leaving you, just changing position."

He replants himself against her eager labia, his large, shiny crown resting against her swollen love lips. Wet and moist, the insurgency plan was easy. Push, slip, slide all the way in, up to his aching balls, he is throbbing and eager to be up tight against her pink velvet. He is still hard, flush against her bushy Venus mound.

Just staying there, luxuriating in his swollen agile rod deep within her gorgeous, sensual body, Paen could just feel himself grow, expand, just by being in physical contact with Nefatia. Feeling even more violatile and explosive as he impregnates her receptive haven. She is all wet, overcome, I mark my approval, as all her exertions make me want to cum - which I finally do. Erupting, a torrent engulfs her wanton body. It is always a joy to copulate with the woman I am coupled with.

“Nefatia, that was truly splendid, amazing. I adore your divine, spirited body.”

“I love the heat from your explosive, rampant manhood, Paen, when all your energy is released into me.”

Avicia comes up to me, fondling my staff, rubbing and massaging, “I see you are still longing for it. Let me have a go at finishing you Paen.”

“My flower I am all yours, please.”

Avicia handles him with authority and diligence, perhaps a little roughly. Squeezing his sac, she pulls and jolts him, jerking in short sharp strokes, she rejuvenates its energy, its hardness. But it excels, watching it thicken, elongate, pulsing hard, as it lays in her hand. She kneels on the bed and turns on her back, Paen above her. She grabs his rigid weapon, placing it between her heaving bosom. Wrapping them around his bulging cockhead, she rubs teases it with her soft flesh. He rides above her, sliding himself backwards, forwards between those two teasing mounds of absolute joy. His throbbing length is just close enough for her to tease him with her hungry tongue.

She flips him over onto his back, straddles his rising pole, then commits all her energy to finishing him off. She rides him extremely hard, ravaging Paen and exerting all her power on his rampant manhood. Using her vaginal muscles, she really squeezes his rotund organ, buried inside her.

“He is all yours, my beauty.”

Erupting, his milk gushes into her. His hot, sticky sediment pleasures her completely overfilling and flowing between both their carnally satisfied selves.

Now it is time for bed. To sleep with, is far too much for one man in a single night. But it feels so good, who can ever refuse them anything?

Awoken by a knock at the door, Paen goes to answer.

"Breakfast is ready young man. If you would all care to join me."

They all go together, partaking of a superb meal before saying their goodbyes.

"Mistress, here is something to remember us by."

Nefatia gives her a bright light blue, satin scarf. Not sure what to do with it, Nefatia puts it around her neck, tying a little knot to secure it in place. Rubbing her neck against it she feels the lightness, the exquisite softness she is overwhelmed by its beauty. She kisses them all and hugs them, not wanting to let them go.

"Thank you so much, it has been a pleasure. If you pass this way again, call in. My door will always be open to you, my friends."

The horse and cart awaits the two ladies mount. Pushing on forward they shout their farewells as they go. Coming across the town quickly, a large church stationed in the middle catches their undivided attention. Again it is Avicia that does the calling as well as the talking. But the two priests that come to the door are unable to help her. They tell her she would be better off going to the city. There are more people there, therefore more chance of finding him, or of someone knowing of him. Try Lincoln, it has a Cathedral, a lot of people. If as you say, the priest as well as the dean led you here, then the dean would have been commissioned at the Cathedral, anyway. So he should lead you back there.

So go there, work backwards from that point. Avicia goes back and reveals the information given to her by the two priests. So they all agree that Lincoln is the place to be. So with their heads down, with a target now in sight, they travel headlong into the hustle and bustle of life that is the city of Lincoln. Not shying away from the problem, that started this journey. Even more reason to be wary, to be cautious of who is watching, following and thinking they can take what is yours. They don't make the quickest headway with their cart. But it eludes suspicion, it's easier to protect and it saves the two women walking.

Paen is out in the wilds, making sure they are all safe and well-protected from any rascals, ruffians or vagrants. Between the three of them, there really is an impregnable, impenetrable ring that keeps them safe from harm, from any infliction or destructive force that may want to disrupt them, to split them up.

The mistress from the farm gave them provisions along with other odds and ends, hopefully to see them through their ordeal. Thus they made their way to the great metropolis that is Lincoln, very wary of what they may encounter there or even, during their travels, to get there in one piece. But there they must go, almost blindly, in the search for a single man, for a single explanation in the hope of curtailing this use of sacrilegious redemption for someone's own vigorous ends.

Most of the farms they used as wayside stops were all deserted; still the threesome salvaged, procuring what they could for their onward journey, to make their lonely lives on the road easier. That way they did not have to trouble or bother anyone else. Also. It avoided drawing attention to themselves. Just in case they unwittingly scare off, the one single person, they wish to talk to. Whenever they stopped, it was always a deserted homestead or an old derelict barn, a dilapidated outhouse or some empty stable block. If need be Paen would erect an awning of sorts over the cart, to keep the inclement weather from the two genteel ladies in his company. Whereas he, because of his hirsute body, was able to keep his body warmth within himself, no matter what the weather.

The villages and hamlets pass them by. They pass through dells, valley, hills, leas and across meadows, through woods and around copses and scrub. Avoiding verges, they pass no other pedestrians, carts or covered wagons. A lonely journey it has been and it's continuing to be so.

Paen does a quick sortie, making an excursion forward. He comes across a recently deserted farmstead. It still looks lived in. Searching the outside area, the werewolf comes across nothing that would tell you why it has been left in such a hurry. There is no livestock, only some tools at the small forge. Entering the farm house, he ran straight away into the smell of death, of rotting corpses. White flesh is turning black, due to the plague. He scrapes out a shallow grave, but deep enough to bury two decomposed bodies. That done, he walks through to the pantry, finding various pottages. Starting a fire, he heats up the remnants of a vegetable soup. Three loaves of bread prove to be edible. A couple of cheeses and some fresh chicken flesh also gets tossed into the vegetable soup. In the barn are a few apples, pears and damsons, which he puts on the table. So all signs of the old family are now gone

He finds a few jugs filled with ale, mead, wine and cider, all added to the large table. He lopes back to the oncoming cart, which is not too far away.

"Nefatia, Avicia I have found somewhere to stay. It is the next farm down. So turn in here, you will see the homestead in front of you."

He rides on the cart in his metamorphosed state. Halting outside the main entrance, they all go in. The heat from the fire has everything warm, homely, comfortable. The chicken and vegetable soup is hot and ready to be consumed. The smell being absorbed by the whole dwelling. Paen goes out to unhitch the horse, filling the trough and letting him run free in the meadows.

Then he makes his way back to the table. Everything ready, table set, Nefatia and Avicia share a jug of wine. Both smile as Paen makes his entrance.

"I see you have got everything ready, for us Paen."

"Yes my goddess, fortunately it did not take up too much time."

"This wine is exceptional. We saved the ale and mead for you, Paen."

"Avicia, I will drink or eat whatever you leave for me. I am a scavenger at heart, anyway."

They sit around the fire, chatting and keeping one another's spirits up with a fortified meal. Probably with some left over, to restock their larder. As well as claiming the tools from the forge. They all enjoyed the banquet and the idle conversation. They reassured one another all tainted with doubts and about coming this far into their quest to discover what is hidden by the devious plot. So the fire is doused. The two ladies make their way to the bedchamber.

Already changed into his alter-ego, he is outside, checking on their safety. He pries deep into the night, yet not a single sound is to be heard, human or animal. But come the glorious dead of night, there is movement, further down the way. Paen whips down to the byway. There, slowly heading towards the farm, is an enraged gang of would-be looters, hoping to find something of value, whether food or even just somewhere to stay for the duration of the night. But all are armed with axes, scythes and pitchforks, aggressive and aggrieved by the collapse of the community they were once part of. Sidestepping, bounding around, then coming from behind them. Before they have a chance to weld, use, or even prepare to protect themselves with their puny weapons. The werewolf jumps all of them, striking all of them in turn. A flash of silver rips their throats asunder. Death comes instantly thankfully, as five mortal souls lie before him, all in the prone position. He just leaves them there to rot, nearly decapitated so there is no chance of them ever rising again. Some more shuffling, then four bodies quietly walking; oblivious to one another; all walking in the same direction. Two women youngish, one middle-aged man, one very old woman, not talking; like moths to an open flame. All following something, or a command of some sort. All being led, by some internal instinct.

Paen just tails them, leaving a gap between the four and himself, slowly and with great purpose. They stop at the edge of the town, waiting, as if needing to be directed somewhere. Then they head directly towards the church, which is just on the downward slope, into the town. The door is opened for them. As they enter they each take a pew. The elderly looking man then goes to the centre of the church, casting his arms to the heavens. A hollow voice booms out from between his open lips, a voice that casts aspersions upon a soul named Bishop John Gynwell. On how he has fornicated and debauched his life away with relatives of those now gathered here. How he had led these young women into sin. How some had died, those he had made pregnant, had been taken into the arms of the nuns. The two he has now. Asking if they require retribution for his sins, as well as sinning against these women; as a leading member of the Catholic church. The shadow sneaks in, acquiring the acolyte.

The congregation remain seated in the deserted, defunct auditorium. The wolf and the man make off as quickly as possible to their hideaway to share his newfound culprit with the psychic and the noble goddess. Leaving him alone, casting his long sermon only to himself, Paen disturbs the sleeping beauties and tells them of his travels, his discovery. He has brought back another body, he says, for Avicia to interrogate. To push him to her limits they both come at once, amazed at the strength of his voice, the power of his speech and diction. Both stand naked, listening to his story, his commands. The seer steps forward, "Yes, this is the one. The face the dean offered up to me, so long ago."

She applies her fingertips to either side of his face, pushing hard as though she wanted to penetrate his skin, to get underneath and to reveal his deepest thought. This did not stem, slow down or stop his rhetoric, nor was it his final command, "Seek John Gynwell at Lincoln Cathedral. Confront him with his mortal, nay sacrilegious sins. A man of the cloth should be exposed and defrocked, revealing what he is. Go now, go forth find him!"

"Yes I have a face. So easily recognizable. For the first time, we have a face to go with the name." Avicia claims loudly.

"So we can all go back to sleep. We have work to do in the morning." Paen says in response to Avicia's loud outburst.

Nefatia of the Sisterhood; her sword sings its song once again. It knows it is about to taste blood, quenching its thirst yet again. Heartbreaker only desires to please and to satisfy his goddess. It is his greatest pleasure! His own lust for blood is only secondary to a satisfactory end. So once again, another servile mortal is split in half. His legs buckle as his tired torso crumples under the terrible infliction, of the crazed power and strength of Nefatia. With a sword sharper than a razor, she cuts through the rib cage, the hypnotic song *Heartbreaker* resounds as he tastes the torment of a fresh kill. Nefatia is on her hands and knees, her face buried in the corpse as she eats the heart as it slowly stops beating. Her long, lashing tongue laps and drinks the thick, red glutinous blood as it congeals. The meal complete, her hair on flame, burning red, white. Glowing like fierce embers. Her eyes wide open, red, a searing scarlet. The song of the victor! Once again she sings the song of the Sisterhood. Paen and Avicia leave her to the acclamation she deserves. Her sword song stops only once her battle dirge ceases. She sings to the music of her beloved sword. Having mutated to fully twice her size, she shrinks back to her normal magnificence. She smiles to the others, "I offer no apology. These infiltrators of reality should not live amongst us."

"We do not require an apology, goddess," Avicia replies.

Paen adds, "We only step back, as a mark of respect for you and Heartbreaker."

"Then I thank you both kindly from my heart. I know you are both my true friends and will be forever more."

# CHAPTER SEVENTEEN

The archdeacon slowly sees his small world crumble, fall apart before him. Now he knows that, with only the Bishop left, as his last protector; his last acolyte, he needs to go to his Crypt. Forced into his final onslaught a lot sooner than he had anticipated, he bestows upon the Bishop added powers over the congregation at the deserted church as they slowly made their way towards the unknowing John Gynwell.

The archbishop of Canterbury, John de Stratford with his retinue of clerics and holy escort, made their way from Ely Cathedral to the safety, protection and security of the moated castle that was once home to the Earl of Rutland. So he could talk at some length with Edward III. He stops to say grace, giving blessings and celebrating the Holy Mass as he went

Bishop John Gynwell is so lost in his fantasy world of sex with the two charming girls at his complete disposal. He has probably completely forgotten that the Cardinal was so close. But at this precise moment in time he was more disposed towards Amora. But when Malyna was left to her own devices, she had found the affections of a younger priest much more to her liking so she spent time with him. She teaches him what men liked. What women liked, their preferences, their ideals. As she did not want to do all the work, like she had been doing with the older

Bishop. For a change she needed to be satisfied, her desires fulfilled, to have a climax given to her by a man. She wanted to be consumed by its entirety.

Amora loved to be on top. She was there now, enjoying the strength of John's erect staff. He sat up, his will and mental capability being over-ridden by the archdeacon the Necromancer. Withdrawing from Amora,

"Excuse me, my dear. I have something I need to do. I will be back as soon as I can."

Dressing in his informal clothes, he makes his way down to the Cathedral. He stands at the door, which is open wide and waits patiently, so patiently.

The archdeacon consoles himself that his future plans are not in complete disarray, it's not yet over. As he makes his way down the vaults to his crypt, he finds the contract still there, embedded deep into the marble of his small private altar. A necromancer of such fine skills so artful, never entertained the thought of giving up or capitulating; not after all these years of graft and fortitude of rendering other people's skills in the dark arts. He, the Necromancer, had left the best to the very end - which would be about now. So his legacy would start this very minute. Laying claim to the English crown. As well as becoming head of church, both at the same time. To usurp the crown of Edward III, the regal crown of this blessed England. To become its majesty, by way of regicide. Also, procure the governance of the church, with all its power, glory and benevolence. To enhance his life, to rise above the salt. To change how this country is run, by the royalty, ministers of the grand old church, along with its corrupt clerics.

The church is run by debauched, over-privileged ministers, who have little thought for their priests, or parishioners. The royalty who have little consideration for the general populace, unless they can add coin or any other physical value to the king's coffers. All poverty relating to both of these hierarchal establishments. The archdeacon dons his all-black attire. The only light is from two small candles, flickering above his altar.

# CHAPTER EIGHTEEN

Paen is racing along to the defunct church on the outskirts of Lincoln. Hoping they are not too late to stop the congregation from leaving its safety, he gets there - yet all to no avail. The church is empty, yet there is not a soul there, nothing there to help in anyway at all. So with the horse and cart, the seer and goddess are not able to keep up with him. Yet they can only keep moving, rumbling along, as quickly as they could.

The Necromancer could sense something, someone, a strange entity coming his way. It is some being he had not encountered before along his many and varied travels, his research. He loses no time.

After his long wait Bishop Gynwell saw his guests approaching. He waves them forward as their bodies were unable to travel faster than they were already were.

Paen makes his appearance just in time and stands behind the gathering. Sunrise was just about to happen; the city lies still, quiet and foreboding. John Gynwell, a lone figure, is on the steps of the Cathedral. The group of miscreants could lead to all sorts of problems. But the werewolf at his most robust takes a chance, expanding his robust, magnificent chest he scoops up the walking dead. Putting them tight against his upper torso, he squeezes with both forearms. Thus he pushes them, extinguishing the life force within each and every body. He breaks all the major bones that make the carcasses walk upright. Dropping them to the floor, he transfigures back to Paen and calls the cart over, "Is this the face you saw as John Gynwell, Avicia?"

"Yes, that is the man Paen."

"Then take him in the cart, to the empty church outside the city limits. See what information you can glean from him."

"OK, I will take Nefatia. Come with me, goddess."

So off they both go. Finding the peace, solitude with no-one to bother them. Sitting the Bishop comfortably at the front of the church, in front of the altar. Placing her hands on the top of his head, they slide them down, covering his whole head. All his prattling's have ceased, forcing her fingertips down. Applying heavy, penetrating pressure makes his eyes sink a little. She sees, senses, feels as she penetrates deeper, forcing the information from him. A clear bright face reveals dark, uncivil, impenetrable, devilish eyes. Instead of mentally revealing a name, he speaks out loud, shouting, "The man you can sense here with me is my archdeacon at Lincoln Cathedral. He is John de Offord."

# CHAPTER NINETEEN

The archdeacon now realizes he is totally alone, that all his acolytes are extinguished. The relatives of the misused, dead, ill-treated young women, all returned to the land of the dead and their afterlife; totally dependent upon their personal beliefs.

So now it is time for the big guns. He has his final incantation to offer to his master. So the Necromancer in his barren enclave will have his chant laid before him. His only light comes from two candles as, at last, his contract has just one signature missing from it. That is his!

So making himself ready, he squints as he starts to celebrate, to sing his chant. It has to be in Latin, repeated three times. Extinguish the candles. Then his all-important audience with his master.

*"Deus tenebris*
*Dominus labarynthe*
*trans exaudi me vacuum*
*Terrorem guile invocabo*
*nos transferre et*
*mortuorum animas vacante*
*vacuous odio*
*hic mihi."*

Then repeated at a louder insistence,

*"Deus tenebris*
*Dominus labarynthe*
*trans exaudi me vacuum*
*Terrorem guile invocabo*
*nos transferre et*
*mortuorum animas vacante*
*vacuous odio*
*hic mihi"*

Finally, at the top of his voice so his master can hear him whereever he may be,

*"Deus tenebris*
*Dominus labarynthe*
*trans exaudi me vacuum*
*Terrorem guile invocabo*
*nos transferre et*
*mortuorum animas vacante*
*vacuous odio*
*hic mihi."*

# TRANSLATION

God of the dark
Lord of the Labyrinth
hear me from across
the void.
I call upon your
dread and guile;
transport your dead valiant souls
of vacuous hate
down here to me.

Immediately he dowses the candles with his thumb and forefinger. Then, just waiting within his own world, the Necromancer waits, lingering in the hush, the dark and damp, the cold of his realm of his enclave, his place of private worship. His chance of immortality. His right to wear the crown, as King of England. His right to lead all the commoners into a new church. A new start, a new religion. To dislodge Edward III and get rid of his cronies, hangers-on, freeloaders, interlopers and carpetbaggers. For him to engage with his people, whilst a coronation would brighten up everyone's life. He can tell the undercurrent, a completely different deity. No wind, no divine intervention, no fanfare, no heralds, just a darkness and the stench. Just appearing, just arriving, just being there, unannounced. Larger than life, he just appears! He takes up the complete volume of the crypt and surrounding vaults.

"Who calls upon Kashaya?"

"I do Master, your Necromancer. One that is not worthy of your thoughts."

"Why do you call upon me at this hour?"

"I need your allies to combat an interloper. Someone who is interfering with our plans, with my strategy."

"Then this means your total commitment to me. You must be subservient for the time I let you serve me. In your lifetime you will honour no one else."

"Yes Master."

"Then your signature with your blood, on your contract. Then you are mine totally."

"I am in your hands. I am part of you as from this moment."

"Then it shall be done ."

Kashpaya breathes upon the archdeacon, his cold stagnant breath absorbed by the Necromancer. Affecting his skin, his whole aura, his whole nature changed. No longer John de Offord, he became but a mere extension of, a serf or pawn, a digit of Kashpaya.

"With this breath I grant you all the assistance you need. My legions will be yours to command, as though I were commanding them myself."

With that the archdeacon felt an instant surge of power, fortitude, resilience, wisdom and universal knowledge drown him. Far beyond his own mental capability come visions of hordes, battalions of unknown wretches, spectres and creatures from the netherworld, from the bosom of the darkness of lost worlds; lost creatures in the wilderness, the forlorn stretching for miles, in front of him. He recognised some forms before him; The Golem from Jewish folklore, Danavas white and black gods and demons, a connection with the waters of heaven prior to the seation from Vectic legend. Dybbuk, a Jewish connection, a malicious possessing spirit believed to be the dislocated soul of a dead person. The Daitya, the female children of Diti, a race of giants from Hindism. The Jotun from Norse mythology, an entity contrasted with gods, often refered to as risi, Thurus and Troll. Then Valkyrie angels of the dead from the same beliefs as the Jotun. Then the compelling cockatrice, a two legged dragon with a rooster's head. They were all looking at him, waiting for his command, his single leadership and direction. The pain of destruction, the pleasure of chaos, death, pain at their hands. In return for an eternal life of heart-rendering misery, torture and very articulate pain; no idea that there is something better out there.

John de Offord sallies forth with his army fully behind him. Leaving his dark, soulless crypt he advances through the damp, dark and foreboding labyrinth of vaults and up through the belly of the Cathedral, out into its perfect auditorium. Out past the vast entrance, that is its wooden doors, they flow down the steps into the speckled sunlight of an English city. His grotesque protectors gather around him. Everyone stops in their tracks, never having seen anything like this before. Not daring to approach, he stated, to all and sundry "No one need get involved. This is for your salvation. I do this to protect you from the likes of the king and the blasphemous church. They who no longer care about the people, the labourer, farmer, wheelwright, smith or the tradesman. They are absorbed with their own lives. They only care about themselves and their debauched, frivolous and carefree lives. The church as well as the crown have lost everyone's respect. The country is falling apart at the seams; some disease is wreaking havoc in every corner of this once free, green and generous land. But fortune, regard and privilege only reverts around the few. For so long, it has been so. Hope itself is no longer held in high regard, as the people die and no one seems to care

The archdeacon carries himself forward, away from the now large crowd that has gathered during his speech. He directed his charges to fully cloak the Cathedral with their harsh, spiritual force. Then he moves out along the main track, out of the city, seeing the disfigured, dismantled bodies he had resurrected to help with his wayward cause; now they lay wasted, useless, cast aside by an unknown enemy of the usurper. He knows he has protection behind him as he approaches the empty, unused church. So it is as solitary barren and undignified as when he first found it, when he decided to make use of it for his desperate cause.

# CHAPTER TWENTY

Paen, Nefatia and Avicia have parked their cart at the other end of town. Walking back in towards the looming, atmospheric Cathedral, they look aloft to see all the strange guardians scattered all over this magnificent church. With no sign of the necromancer apparent, Avicia seats herself on the steps of the astounding building enamored with its beauty, presence and workmanship. The other two venture into the Cathedral, accosted by some of the guardians; but these are soon disposed of as Paen turns into the hungry werewolf form and the goddess unsheaves her mighty heartbreaker. Looking, delving, acting as insurgents; as the protecting forces watch quietly, they look for any display of disruption or upheaval, so they can protect this from the enemy of their lord.

Paen checks for hidden stairways, steps or back passages, trying to find a way to the top. Nefatia checks all the other rooms for anything or anyone that might be able assist in finding the archdeacon. Slowly Paen rootes out the hidden stairways that enable him to scale the heights to the acme of the building, this superb architectural masterpiece.

The goddess hears a little giggling coming from one of the rooms. Going in, she finds it empty. But there is an interconnecting door. This she unlocks, then opens the door.

There before her are two naked bodies. Amora and Malyna are pursuing each other's pleasures, sucking each other's erect nipples.

"Ladies, I hope you are enjoying each other to the full. I do not want to disturb or interrupt, but could you tell me if the archdeacon is about?"

"No, he has left, that was some time ago now," Malyna tells her.

"But we do not know where he was going," Amora adds, quite sure of herself.

"Thank you for your time," Nefatia smiles.

She leaves, allowing the two youngsters to get back to their personal games.

Paen reaches the pinnacle of the Cathedral so he can look across the vast city. He can see clearly across the whole inter-locking terrain. Something he could neither understand nor comprehend. That was how far the land stretched before him; yet on the ground he could see view next to nothing. It was like a dream, seeing everything all in one go. All too much in this tiny world. He found his way down again. Approaching the steps, he finds Avicia still sat there.

"I have not found any sign of him at all, Avicia."

"Where is Nefatia?"

"She went searching the rooms."

"Did you see any young women while you searched the Cathedral?"

"None at all."

"I have a feeling, that the two females will not be safe up there on their own. We need to care for them, until they are found by their immediate relatives."

"We wait for Nefatia first. Then we ask her if she seen any young girls."

"Then we wait for Nefatia, Paen." Avicia replies.

"The Archdeacon is not here, at the Cathedral, so I have been informed." Nefatia tells both Avicia and Paen.

"Nefatia, did you see any young girls in any of the chambers?" Avicia asks her sister.

"Yes Avicia. There were two of them alone in the Bishop's chambers. They seemed to be waiting for someone, but they were enjoying each other's company. They seemed to know each other very well. If they were waiting for the Bishop's return, they will have a rather long wait ahead of them."

"Nefatia, one of them should not be here. She is the Earl of Rutland's niece. The other is the Bishop's courtesan. I think we need to get both of them out of here, just in case something happens."

"OK, we all go in. You two take care of the young women. I will keep the way clear."

As Paen turns into his alter-ego, the two women follow on behind him, feeling the safest they can behind his immense bulk.

"I think they must only be about sixteen. So young to be led astray," Nefatia says in passing,

"It is sad. But that is the church of today, debauched and without religion," Avicia adds.

"Paen, you stay here. We will bring the two maidens back with us," the two women tell him, together.

Avicia and Nefatia go back into the Cathedral, back into the chambers where Nefatia first found the two girls. Now the two of them were fast asleep on the plush velvet, very soft double bed of the Bishop. They each go to a side, gently shaking the two young maidens.

Slowly they awaken.

"What are your names, young ladies?" Avicia asks, as they rise and work out where they are.

"I am Amora, the niece of the Earl of Rutland. This is Malyna, my very dear and close friend, the daughter of the Cathedral's cook. We have been waiting for the Bishop!"

"We are very sorry to have to tell you that he will not be returning. We just want to make sure you are both kept safe," Nefatia tells them.

"So would you both get dressed, so we can take you with us?" Avicia explains, softly.

"Yes mistress, we will come with you now." Malyna smiles, loving the company of other women, feeling good and secure with them.

In his werewolf form, Paem is patrolling the passageways, sniffing out any problems that might come their way, or disturb them in one way or another. But there is nothing whatsoever. The two young maids, both dressed in Malyna's finery, are escorted out of their chambers by the two adult women, here to save them.

Paen waits for them very patiently and then tells them, "Come, come ladies, let us go to the outside where we will be safe. The person we are looking for cannot be found. Use our cart as a safe haven for now. I will go looking for him."

"Malyna, Amora, this is Paen, another one of us. Trying hard to make everything safe, for all of us."

They all smile and nod to one another as he disappears.

The Earl, along with the King, the Cardinal, his wife and his own retinue of guards, approach his castle, hearing that an emissary has arrived from Bolougne with news of his, daughter. They ride straight up to the castle, into its confines, as a stronghold to receive the news.

Paen makes his way out of town, back towards the deserted church where they had left the Bishop. Unbeknown to Paen, Nefatia had been trailing him with Heartbreaker at her side, within his scabbard constantly until he was required. Avicia stayed at the cart with the two young women, awaiting assistance. She sensed something was coming her way. She saw the heavy floom, the trail of dust, approaching.

# CHAPTER TWENTY-ONE

The archdeacon, John de Offord, could sense the two transgressors coming his way. He could see the mounted troops in the distance, the Earls personal bodyguard. Entering the town from the other side. Dispatching the cathedral guardians immediately to dispose not only the troops, but also the King, Cardinal and the Earl along with anyone else in that party.

Whilst at the church, without any deliberation, the Necromancer sent forth the despicable apocalypse of his own making, for his own self-contrived purposes. Once started this will not stop, cannot stop, until the end result is achieved. Or when the Necromancer is completely destroyed and disposed of. He sends them out to vanquish the personal guard of the Earl. But the imposing figure of the werewolf with both Avicia and her sister, Nefatia sitting astride his broad back, having collected both of them previously, goes out to defend the King, Cardinal and the Earl. As the swathes of golems and danavas hurtle down from above, Paen's alter-ego extends his proportions, enabling him to fight the dispossessed within their own sphere of conflict. He with his teeth bared. long savage; his elongated claws, brutal lashing across the bodies of the demons. Combating these beasts from the netherworld. He lured in the werewolf with all his power to fight them with such brutal savagery, learnt from his time with the she-wolf he skirmishes within their own dimension. Against the odds he keeps them at bay, away from the company; so the royal party passes through safely, unscathed.

Coming back into the realm of his own reality, Paentells his two comrades-in-arms to try and find the perpetrator of this uncontrollable hazard, which would at this moment in time seems even worse, more detrimental than the ensuing plague. They both get a ride once again on his back, to the horse and cart.

"You both be careful, wary and keep *Heartbreaker* very close Nefatia, to hand if need be."

"We will Paen, Heartbreaker sings your name in jubilation. See you soon."

So Avicia with Nefatia head out to the other end of town, the goddess taking the reins. Avicia puts out her feelers trying to locate the heretic, causing this serious rebellion within the church, along with the attempt to usurp the crown. So coming to a stop outside the Cathedral, the syblis tentively getting off the cart and feeling her way around the supposedly empty building. Her sensitive, receptive senses tell her there is still no one here, or even close.

"Nefatia, the Cathedral is still empty. So we need to search further. We need to travel slowly, tread carefully. I am sure we will come across what we need, what we are looking for, as long as we stay patient."

She gets back onto the cart, not only sensing but physically looking. Four pairs of eyes are looking, seeking for anything, anyone. The syblis, the goddess both using their special talents as a syblis and vampire to make sure their safety is not compromised. Malyna peering out of the back, just in case a single thing is missed. A cockatrice mounted by a Dybbuk right on top of the two young maidens, at the back of the cart.

"Mistress, mistress Avicia, Nefatia, did you see that beast with a rider on his back flying through the sky?"

"Where, where Malyna?" asks Nefatia.

"Here, at the back of the cart." Replies Amora.

"Probably part of his protection, safeguard, starts here dear sister." Avicia points out to her sister, Nefatia.

Avicia dismounts, standing to the side. She looks about her and waits, needing him to display himself once again. Amora shouts as loud as she can, in warning, "There, there! Coming towards us."

She looks upwards, back behind her. There, coming towards them, brace of cockatrice, one with a wraith as a rider, a tormentor. The other one mounted by the Dybbuk, here to disrupt and cause chaos within mankind. Whenever he is called from the depths, he is a wilful protagonist, spiteful, mean and uncaring.

But Avicia puts her hands up and out, just as the claws pass through her. She can sense that their skilled adversary is very close by. He is outside the city. Not too far away, close enough to get to. She keeps her focus pinpointed, her vision to mind. As they venture forward with their horse and cart, the deeper they get into the necromancer's territory, the stronger the defences. All strange manner of visions spectacles and dreams arise from the earth, or descend from the bilious. They were a thousand fold, a fierce onslaught of virile barbarians, spectres and phantoms.

Avicia applies herself to calling the werewolf, who is Paen to come to their aid. The affinity between the two lovers had always been strong. But the bond had only gained strength and depth, importance and longevity over the years as they got to know each other, physically, mentally and sexually. One only had to think of the other, the thought traversing across the ether, for either of them to find the other.

But he felt rather than heard her call from afar, from her mind. He knew neither bounds nor shackles, no restrictions that would stop him, to get to her in her time of dire need. To avail himself to her safety, security, her vulnerability. He finished the battle with the golems, danavas. He had nearly overstretched himself but had put them on the run in his eagerness to dislodge all of them at the same time. Disrupting their party in the sky he took them on a little at a time, slowly annihilating them in small bands. Their attempts, to annul, to unceremoniously disable any of the three nobles, within the royal party.

Stopping for nothing and no one he hastened to be at the side of his beloved Avicia in her time of grief, woe, forbearance, trouble, solitude.

The presence that is the might and power of the werewolf stands there, at the breech outside the city, eyeing the sky. The necromancer still not disclosing his hideaway, his whereabouts. The three stand alongside the horse and cart, looking up at the vast torrent of minions holding their place in the abundant heavens.

"Nefatia take Avicia, Malyna and Amora. Go search for the person, individual, the thing that you are after. I am going to take the force of this blight upon myself."

"OK, we are going. But first I will take the two girls to the royal escort, to be looked after."

The archdeacon pushes his forces, his army of belligerent thugs, forward. All the hustling and bustling as they come ever nearer, closer to the werewolf. All the legions of the Necromancer's allies approach and advance onto the menance who is Paen in his Werewolf totally. All manner of threshing maniacs, all revelling for the confrontation here and now. Yet there is not a single mounted adversary. They are all foot soldiers, all in step as they march onto the open leas and meadows outside the city. The werewolf totally immersed himself in the conflict before him. He races in, changes his size, as he marauds through the ranks, disconcerting them even as they advance upon him.

Avicia sense that her quarry is further out of town. After giving the two young maidens into the custody of the Earl, she drives out into the suburbs of the city, seeing the deserted church they had forgotten about, out into the distance.

"Nefatia, come on. I think we need to make our way over to the church. That one, over there, all by itself."

The royal escort make their way to the edge of the city, to be totally amazed at the ranks that awaited them. Held at bay by a single, unwavering silver-coloured wolf that was wading in amongst them. All these fantastic beasts, ogres and phantoms of myth, legend and folklore are all here fighting under the leadership of man: a high-voltage necromancer who can control his forces, his army, without necessarily seeing them.

The king's escort battles on the ground, with this formidable force, this physical foe. Swords are striking and piercing but not actually penetrating the actual being. The Werewolf rears up on his hind legs, his jowls clamping down on the front ranks of the golems, danavas and dybbuk. It is they that get torn, shredded and ripped from their immediate ranks. The King's guard trying to help, some dismounted, flaying their swords against the apparitions. Some of the archers shoot their longbows and crossbows heavenward. Nearly all make their mark. Some of the spirits fade, falling or vanishing; then all too soon they rise again fronting the queue, to get their hands on the invading werewolf.

The blooded werewolf was evading their clutches; but slowly reducing their numbers. Using his claws and teeth, his jaws emitted his hot, vile dog's breath, the snot, saliva and the searing burning energy from his large amber eyes. Fearsome he is, but even more so as he gains strength from these enemies before him, who try to conquer him, debase him. But he absorbs, infuses their power, strength and density. He increases his own longevity, his aura and mortality; his ability to survive and to overcome.

Nefatia enters the church, going to the left-hand side and, into the presbytery. There beneath her feet she finds a trapdoor. Quietly Avicia pulls it up, opens it. She sees straight away, beyond the blinding light. The necromancer.

"Nefatia, he is down here! The one we have been after; he's causing all the chaos all the disruption. Go very careful if you're down there, he'll be alert to whatever happens in his own realm, and this one."

"OK Avicia, but you keep out of harm's way. You stay here, I only want to have to deal with him. I want to know that you're secure so that I don't have to worry about you as well. I have no way of knowing what will happen once I confront him, one on one."

Nefatia scales down the into the vaults of the dilapidated, deserted church. It was small, but the vaults were huge in comparison. The silence and the dark filled all her senses as she moved slowly, warily; feeling her way forward. There was a thin cord, a bond of connection with her delicate sister, Avicia. She was her guide, directing her along the dank and slimy walls.

His size Grew relentlessly as Paen demolished everything placed in front of him. The forces of dread, ill-will and darkness growing impatient, more reckless and more gung-ho. The wolf composed himself, increasing power and strength, in energy and size, at the behest, annoyance, of the struggling pawns in this fight. Aided in the real world, protecting as much as they were able, with what they had with them, with what they had to hand. For which the Paen is more than thankful. The hordes fall back to the outskirts of the bewildered city. Now relentlessly they protect the church and its grounds. Paen growls, his hot putrid breath forcing the army of the netherworld backwards.

Nefatia is alert, Heartbreaker roused in her hand to protect her face as he sings her name relentlessly. Filling her with awe, the sword summons inspiration, making her blood boil. Then finally comes the light, a coruscation as the crypt unfolds. There he is! An imprecation is in progress, a sonorous intonation:

*"Contabo fortitudinem*
*Belial Beelzebub habet et;*
*De his qui invocal*
*STYGIUS INPOTENTIA*
*ACARDIAC.*
*PROBROSUS INIQUUS.*
*INCENDIUM*
*Unicum Salvatorem."*
*TRANSLATION:*
*"Sing of the might of*
*Belial and Beelzebub;*
*They who invoked the*
*Stygian despotism*
*acardiac.*
*Nefarious Iniquitous.*
*Perdition*
*my only saviour."*

Dressed in black, his eyes as dark as a void, he is not the archdeacon of old anymore. Not the older, slim man of yore. A stocky, stronger man. Almost his voice is too deep, almost inaudible. His forces are in decline, backing off. He turns to face his challenger.

"Who enters this hallowed place?"

"I, Nefatia first daughter of Queen Neferata. It is I that enters this corrupt den of evil."

"Then face the pain, the anger of Kashpaya, my master."

Nefatia lunges hard with her falchion. Heartbreaker whistles past, he can sense his quarry is so very close. She marches forward; blinded by a fork of light, sent her way. Even one on one, it was going to be an awkward battle.

Avicia transcends her body and absorbs the forks of the blinding force. Allowing her sister vampire the vantage, of gaining on the flagitious necromancer. To get close enough for her sister vampire to nibble at his flesh, he pulls his arm back. But too slow, a searing pain wrenches through him as Heartbreaker nicks his forearm. Momentarily losing all his focus, some of his pawns disappear from the grounds, vanquished and defeated immediately. His loss of concentration has cost him his allies, leaving his own power and focus diminished.

The colossus that is the werewolf endorses this fear, wielding his superior lupine anger and strength as he threshes in amongst the remnants of the banshees, golems, danavas, Valkyrie and dybbuk. Now they in turn slowly back off.

Dripping slowly the blood runs from his deep, agonising wound, yet forcing himself to focus he sends forth his last line of defence. Jotun, the giants who did not like the insurgence of the gods, replacing the Jotun as the idols, effigies, deities of the people. Also, at their side, into battle go the Daityas, not willing to wilt before the unbelievers.

The undead, who match them at every point. With even less manpower, than they have, to call upon. Still the resilient werewolf fights them tooth and claw. As they get larger, endowed with their father's power, so does the werewolf. Mounting a single-handed battle, crusade, against the supposed enforcer.

Back in the vaults the sisters are working as one. Now they have him cornered, at their disposal now he neither withdraws nor gives way to anything or anyone. Nefatia displays her swordplay. Heartbreaker whistles as she plays with him.

The werewolf at his most rabid does not elude nor evade anything thrust at him bodily, whether in this dimension or the next. The Daityas thrusting ahead, challenging his power, might and concentration. Their combined pressure infuriates the wolf. Becoming a colossus, vanquishing, eating these tasty morsels; as they surge, charge forward, towards him alone. He does nothing, except wait; taking them as they march imperiously towards him.

Avicia is now inside Nefatia's thoughts, deflecting the force of his curses even as he wields his unworldly energy, strength and power. He grins as his eyes flare, directed solely at the female with the sword. Nefatia used his tactic against him. Heartbreaker's superior reflective surface casts back the force of energy that was aimed at her; now forged a passage through the ether back towards the Necromancer, the virile, despotic and impassable Necromancer. The force exerted was strong enough to disable him, knocking him off balance. The falchion surged in taking Nefatia with him. But as she wields her mighty weapon, thrusting into his torso, Heartbreaker bites into nothing, thin air. The Necromancer is gone in an instant! Nefatia screams aloud, deafening, her sword wailing, the nearest it gets to crying, sobbing.

"Nefatia, Nefatia sister, that was his last line of defence. I think we need to back to the city. To Lincoln Cathedral, we will find him waiting, hiding there."

"Dearest Avicia, get the cart, we will go now. I will tell the lupus albus of our immediate quest as we pass."

Paen the werewolf is enraged by the abundance of kills around him, yet still they come for him. But the Daityas and the giants, the Jotun vanishes, leaving his opposition a little less formidable. He scrubs out the banshees until the danavas back away. But the golem carry on forward towards their foe regardless. Simply because they have nowhere else to go, nothing else to do - apart from fight and die.

Nefatia shouts amid his strife and battling, "Lupus albus! We make haste to the Cathedral, his final hideout, we assume."

The shadow roars defiantly, aggressively, then he is away - bounding ahead, lost to sight so soon. For the first time the two sisters bound along, side by side in the horse and cart, behind the royal escort. All are making apace for the deserted city and it's Cathedral to waylay the usurper, the one intent on regicide. But they are not quick enough. The darkness is consuming the air and the archdeacon is already there. After being discovered earlier, he is ready. His power and energy are focused. His energy vilified; containing his whole body. Entrenched with absolute power, he waits only for the arrival of these unknown insurgents. They had shown themselves, knowing who the enemy was now.

The werewolf already there. Now fully exposed, alone, completely by himself. Already to greet him churlishly, was the jotun, daityas, attempting to flay him straight away. The albino werewolf cornered and at his most dangerous, had his hands full, his mind occupied with the presence of the giants. But at the same time niggled by the children of Diti and Kashpaya. Controlling his temper, although seething with contempt; absorbing the power, matching the size of the jotun, his hunger not sated, nor satisfied. His stature not meek, nor mild. Feisty, the jotun came forward, revealing their true size; the masquerade over. The royal escort look on in disbelief! Stopped dead in their tracks.

The werewolf scathes with the unrelenting close quarter combat, lost in the realms of someone else's fantasy; never capitulating, or even thinking of it; as he fought. No excuse for failure.

The horse and cart rumbles forward to the steps of the Cathedral. The jotun and the daityas were preoccupied with battling with the tireless werewolf. Unable to do anything against the two sisters, they enter the vast interior of the church. The sisters work together; the psychic, feeling, sensing and absorbing the intrusion of the Necromancer. Finding their way down to the vaults. Silently Avicia tries to conceal their entry from the awareness of the darkness. Gently she passes down the stairway to the crypt, a vast open space. Stealth was needed by both maidens.

"Do not violate his space. If we can we come from behind. Surprise him if we can, between us. If not, anyway at all. Both of us, or one of us. You understand, my sister?"

"Avicia, you let me go from the front. That will give you more chance. If I can occupy him fully I may move his focus or direction. But patience, my dearest Avicia. Tell me all that you see or sense. Make it safe for both of us, all the time we are alone here."

Avicia leads the way forward for them both, through the long twilight vaults beneath the cathedral.

The King, Cardinal and the Earl all are outside.

The two women listen as they physically feel their way along the arches, plinths, columns and turns. Avicia stops, closes her eyes and senses her way forward.

Just as he lights the single candle, he senses them both very close. He sees Avicia and tries to put out the lighted candle, but knocks it over!

The werewolf feels overwhelmed by the extreme odds, but fighting nevertheless. He knows he has to keep battling to give the two sisters all the chances they need, all the time they require to direct the Necromancer's focus elsewhere. The werewolf exhales, exhales and exhales. His body is bolstered and energized as his physical appearance towers above the giants. Repelling them, bringing them down.

The Necromancer falters, forgetting there was two. Impetuosity getting the better of his thoughts, he goes for the one he could see. He raised his arm; Nefatia swinging around. Her guardian Heartbreaker as if he had a mind of his own, assails the physical body of the once archdeacon. Just one, lone, single thrust. Severing the flesh from the bone, she disables the Necromancer. Cutting through his entire ribcage. Heartbreaker sings to his heart's content loud and clear as it whistles across the air. The goddess is down on her knees, ripping and tearing the broken, spoilt ribs out of the way.

Her face in amongst the red, warm fluid, that is his blood. Still hot, flowing as he lingers in life. She drinks its life-giving force. Then she tears his dark and devious heart, eating it, gulping it down so it cannot escape her. The pleasure, gratification derived from this is undeniably good, so satisfying. Such is her divine right for annihilating this lost, misbegotten soul.

Lupus albus turns to his next obstacle. There stands Ahriman, a god of powerful proportions, co-existing as a cross between a bull and a sphinx. A cockatrice, a winged serpent, with a vile head of a cockerel. Then there was the fret, an all-encompassing ogre of a giant, ready to defile anything and everything. Finally comes Kashpaya, as one with Lucifer and Belial, a god of no mean presence and demeanour. He turns to the interloper, "I am Kashpaya, a god. I give in to no one, especially not a mere wolf, craving my life, on my own doorstep."

"I am nothing, I am beholden to no one, nothing. My life belongs to the Sisterhood. You and your misbegotten followers do not scare or unsettle me.

Nefatia stands before the decimated body, raising her hands and bloodied face, to the heavens, smiling,

"Victory is mine! I am Nefatia of the sisterhood."

The radiance surrounds her as before.

Her long, thick, lush hair turns to strands of incessant fire, it's fierce, raging flames act as a halo. Her eyes are the red of hate, dark, unforgiving; undisputed revenge. Heartbreaker shouts out her name in defiance, in regal delight and triumph. She roars her name, as she grows in height, width. Nothing compares to her, nothing scares her as she picks up her sister with a single arm. Fleeing the flames that eat away at the altar, crypt and chancel she makes her way to the protection of the horse and cart, as far away from the all engulfing conflagration as possible.

Lupus albus wrangles with all the entourage that Kashpaya had with him. Scrabbling in the dirt, Colossal figures try to obliterate one another.

The werewolf feels an arm trying to garrotte him, so sinking a fang into the offending limb, a touch of acupressure; but he did not know it at the time, a simple process of stopping the flow of blood, by closing an artery with his vile fang. He kept there a while, until the flailing limb ceased, whereupon the Afreet crumpled, fell away and died.

Nefatia appeared unafraid, but called to the cockatrice, that ugly concoction of serpent and cockerel. Its choler oozes from its wide-open jaw. Longing to get involved in the deliberation, it decides to attack the goddess just for good sport, until he could find a way to get into the werewolf. The cockatrice, swooping down, lashes out at the body of Nefatia, but misses as she thrusts her sword upwards.

Kashpaya, seeing it was not all going his way, cast his eyes to the heavens, full of opprobrium. He casts a nefarious imprecation to the winds:

"STO veniet in
latus meum;
ilico."

Translation:

"ACHOR come (Achor, being the god of flies.)
to my side;
this instant."

The unhallowed lupus albus now used a manoeuvre he never knew he could manage. He had thought about it, and it was within the realms of his possibilities he was going to attempt bifurcation. Forking in two, he could surround his quary, then squeezes the very life from him. Ahriman was the god to succumb to this method of finality. The shadow, with immense deliberation, focused and forced his body to split, fork and surround the body of Ahriman. Then he squeezes the very essence of the god from him. He feels the need to emasculate Ahriman, just to ensure he understood who he was dealing with. Ahriman evaporated, dismissed to his own dimension.

Achor arrived with the wind. Eldritch! Bicephalous, he flapped his ornate wings. his two heads moving independently of each other. One, the head of a fly; the other just a face of complete opprobrium, void and inane; it senses feeling only in the abstract, from where he had just come.

At last Nefatia evades the cockatrice's violent manoeuvres. Intrusions aplenty cumbersome with that weight, just a little slow on the return swerve, the goddess is able to decapitate it, slaying the fabulous beast. Slicing down the entire length of the serpent, she smashes the breast of the obnoxious being. Finding both of its hearts beating in time, she wrenches them out, one in each hand, and eats both, amongst the gore and entrails and blood. Then taken aback, on the arrival of the other being. she felt right away a sense of contemn. But she was going through her transformation, as he arrived. Not holding back, directing her sword at this blasphemous being, lord of the filth. She being a pyromancer in league with the power of fire; her ally Heartbreaker at her side, as always. Directing her firepower through the extension of her faithful falchion, directly at Achor. A seething blast of laser-strength force and energy disrupts his very existence as he is blown away, back to his own unearthly world - wherever that was.

The superior lupus albus is still at odds with Kaspaya. This was leading to a truculent impasse, with no blood spilt, or displayed. Both bodies exert so much force, power and combined energy. With unhallowed contempt for what each other stood for, both pairs of hands wrap around each other's necks. Realising that neither was going to win; the werewolf stands his ground. He shouts at Kaspaya, "God, what do you do here? Your enmity, that flagitious spawn of a cesspool, is no longer. He has been vanquished, just like that Achor you called upon. Why don't you go back to your own glade of misadventure, where you are still a god? Here without your necromancer, you are nothing. Avaunt! Or we shall finish this, you will be no victor here in this realm."

The now majestic werewolf ululates, his lungs sending out his message to all and sundry; his howling resounds across the void for an eternity. His composure settles, his blood comes off the boil. The red mist dissipates, vanishes, renders itself neutral once again. There before everyone stands Paen. He walks across to his two sisters, as the great fire burns all that stands in its way; "Are you both unhurt, safe?"

"Yes, my dearest brother. We are both secure, unscathed. The necromancer is nullified.," Avicia tells him, with a broad grin showing on her sweet lips.

"Good, then our work is done. We should make our way back to Riche Mont, away from all this savagery. To rest and recover, and get ourselves back to normal, once again."

# CHAPTER TWENTY-TWO

But as they discuss between them what their next move will be, the Earl William comes into their presence;

"Excuse me kind people, first I would like to thank you all. For saving my niece, along with her very dear friend. Then for protecting us, the King, the Cardinal and myself, from that frantic, inane usurper, along with all the retinue he had with him. Finally, we would like you, all three of you, to attend the dinner tonight, at my castle before you think of returning home, wherever that may be."

"But what of the Cathedral and the raging inferno?" Nefatia asks.

"The King says to let it burn. Perhaps it will rid us of this infernal plague so that we can start afresh. It will leave a scar across the countryside but it will fade and heal in time."

"We were going to look for somewhere to stay overnight, before returning tomorrow. So thank you, we would be more than happy, to join you," Avicia replies.

"In that case follow us to my humble abode."

"Thank you, that is very gracious of you, Sir." Avicia smiles as she returns her answer.

So following on behind the escort at the back with the horse and cart, they follow the lead of the royal retinue. The fire, flames and smoke wrap themselves all over the once magnificent, glorious cathedral at Lincoln. All the stonework crumbs and falls upon itself and all the oxygen exhausted by that single fallen candle, deep down in the crypt. The city is slowly being eaten away by the incendiary aftermath of that fateful light.

As they leave all that, they follow on behind the entourage and royal traffic to the fortified home of the Earl, for safety, the banquet, as well as a good night's sleep. Travelling at twilight, the fire at the Cathedral was the beacon, the lantern showing us the way onwards to the moated castle of Gilbert de Gand. But now it belonged to William de Bohun. They entered, the horse and cart, the final object to enter through the wooden portcullis, it came down, shutting us away from the outside world once again. The horse and cart led round to be stabled. The horse shown into a very impressive stable with all the water he could drink and all the rich oats he could tuck into, while he was here. Nefatia, before she leaves, gives the horse a drink, including a drop of the elixir, to make him a full time member of the team.

The trio is shown to their rooms and chambers. Paen alone, then the two maidens put together, in a large chamber. the two strephons together, relaxed in each other's company. Paen is alone and sleeping after his infernal battle.

The two sisters, Avicia and Nefatia disrobe each other. They clean and wash each other's bodies with her Egyptian soap, with the help of the slightly chilled water. Then, as they look at each other, they come so very close, hugging and kissing. Long forgotten physical touching, passing their hands across, over one another's bodies. The kisses are hard and long, deep and re-assuring, their tongues tasting and stroking as Avicia softly pulls Nefatia's aroused nipples, loving those plump cherries in between her fingers as she toys with them, twisting and squeezing. Nefatia gently caresses Avicia's bosom, tracing and running her eager digits, round and round her uneven aureoles. Moving her long tongue from her sister's lips, she kisses her breasts, licking, running the tip of her tongue once again across and over her coarse aureoles. Then, sucking her upright, juicy teats, she compels them to thicken.

Then Avicia lowers herself to her knees. Placing both her electric lips over her sister's anxious pink velvet, she proceeds to suck, to gorge herself, flicking her oral muscle in between her sister's loins. Pushing in deep, she rubs her greedy tongue up tight against her vaginal walls. She makes her thighs twitch, tremble and succumb as Nefatia's juices run over her open lips, then spills on over down her long firm thighs. Her sister's cream is so sweet, but she is unable to drink all of her.

Nefatia bends down, her body still relishing Avicia's tender touch. Then picking up Avicia, she lays her naked body across their bed. Kneeling over her, she grinds her wet, sticky groin up against the dry, perfect one of her sisters. Then she inserts her finger deep into Avicia's avid, wanton Venus mound. Riding, fingering, sucking, her labia, tormenting her so. Then returning to her excellent mammilla, so juicy. She sucks and pulls them both with her teeth, chewing beyond her endurance. Her glorious thick teats, so juicy, her fingers sticky. The two strephons both overcome with each other's attentions; both sticky, extremely joyful. Finally they clean each other, softly and gentle. Then Nefatia chooses a fine pelisse to wear along with a pair of bluchers, a mantelet, to throw across her shoulders. Her falchion heartbreaker is concealed within the bustier, beneath the pelisse she wore. Avicia dons a camlet bodice, a pair of buskins and a colourful jupe, finished off with a cincture with a capuchin. Very fetching they both looked, too.

They go out hand in hand, knocking on their swain's door.

"Paen, are you ready? Your two sisters are outside waiting for you, to take them to the banquet."

"Avicia, Nefatia, I am coming, for you," calls Paenas the door opens, naked as ever as he steps out. The young maidens take an arm each as he escorts them both to the great hall. The rest of the company is already here, seated. The Earl rises, showing Paen to his seat - below the salt. The two sisters sat in between the Earl's brothers. The wine is passed round and all goblets charged. Earl William raising his, "To our saviours. We thank them all, with all our hearts."

He looks down at the two sisters, "Beauty, grace, a fierce heart and a quick death to you both. We hope you will both join our community. Please, enjoy all we have to offer."

# CHAPTER TWENTY-THREE

"Sire, my liege?" asks a page as he kneels before the king,

"Yes, what is it boy?"

"An envoy from France is here to see you. Andrew Ullford."

"Then send him in immediately," Edward III rises and goes to meet the envoy.

"Andrew, what is it you have to tell me?"

"Sire, perhaps you should hear in this in private."

"No, tell me now, what news do you have for me?"

"Your daughter, Joan, is dead. Taken by the plague, in Bordeaux. She never reached Castile, her whole retinue was taken by the Black Death."

The whole entourage now knew that the most protected woman in Chrisendom was not immune from the Bubonic Plague. The gathering was silent in respect of their king. Not knowing what to say or do to console him. There was nothing that could be done to counteract such a great loss – Edward storming out of the hall mumpich, wanting to be alone. Even Philippa, his wife, was unable to share all his grief and sorrow. Both knew the finality of it all and they'll never be able to see their glorious daughter, Joan, again.

Paen all but forgotten, no matter. The battle was won. So now he moves on, all being well, back to Riche Mont. Feeling more than a little tired and battle-weary, he leaves the revellers to their drinking and stories of bravery, feasting. Quietly he makes his way back to his room. Not wanting to be noticed or caring if he is missed, he just needs to rest and wants to do it now so as to recoup his powers, closing his door behind him. He lays upon his soft bed, sleep coming almost straight away.

Nefatia and Avicia eat, both put off by the continuous touching, petting and advances made by the male courtiers around them. Given no rest, whispering; the wanting of them, bravado shown to try to get their attention. The wanting of them to go with the Earl's brothers for sexual favours. They had noticed Paen leaving early in the proceedings requiring, wanting, needing to leave with him, for their own safety.

Avicia stretches her all-encompassing, agile mind, contacting her erstwhile lover. Whispering to him, she tells him that they both need his help. She gives him a metaphysical kiss, so loving, endearing; breathed his name across his whole mind; ran her fingers through his thick, coarse lupine hair. Paen awoke, afraid he had forgotten all about his two sisters alone, amidst that depraved gathering, fairly sure they could take care of themselves, especially as Nefatia was armed.

Transmuting into the vicious and powerful albino werewolf, softly makes his way to the very busy grand hall.

Nefatia is sitting in between the Earl's two brothers, Avicia on the one side. The goddess was becoming irate, dressed in one of her favourite dresses that reveals every curve of her devilish, substantial body. Both brothers continually touch them both. Mauling and pawing, they transgress the bounds of a friendship, even though there was none to be had. Caressing both their ample charms, they stroke their breasts, their legs, trying to steal kisses from both the tender, sweet, young maidens. One hand too many tries to sneak under her dress; another tries to go over the top of Avicia's, trying to pursue the roundness, firmness of all four glorious orbs. Enough!

She pushed them aside and stood up, "LEAVE US BOTH ALONE," she shouted at the top of her voice.

Nefatia reclaims Heartbreaker which is still strapped to her back in a bustier, beneath her revealing dress. Whistling loudly on its way out of its scabbard. Glistening and glinting as he felt the warmth of the two brothers with two deep thrusts, he lunges thirsty for the quench of blood, once drawn. Splitting both ribcages, he goes down, felling both with equal ferocity. Poleaxing both so violently, she relishes the surge of blood to her lips. That hot vibrant fluid, as it still flows from both brothers as they in turn breathe their last lungful of oxygen. Then she snatches both hearts, just before they die and fade. She gorges on the flaming meat, as fresh as it can be, still hot to the touch, still covered in the sinew, muscle and speckles of blood.

Everyone stood agog, the whole hall silent, as Nefatia finished her elaborate meal; her sister stood at her side sensing knowing that the werewolf was on his way. The whole royal entourage had to recover from the spectacle they had just witnessed. No-one dared to breath or speak out of turn.

The werewolf appears as an apparition; without sound, silent, foreboding and aloof. Rearing up on his hind legs, he reaches for his fullest stature. A royal guard runs at him, ready to hack him with his puny, inoffensive sword. The overwhelming lupus albus, with a single slash of his mighty claw, removes his throat.

Ululate, he does with a vengeance, to break the silence. To let it be known that he will exact a payment from them all, if pushed too far.

Several others get up to fight the wolf. But Edward gets up, shouting to all and sundry. "Let them do as they will! You cannot, will not, are totally unable to stop them. Consider what they did for us, this day. Show some gratitude. the Earl's brothers started this fracas, due to their want of the two young women beside them. It looks to me that they are more than able to protect themselves. SO LEAVE THEM, OR THEY WILL FINISH YOU!"

With that everyone backed off.

The esteemed albino werewolf rescued his two maidens from the general melee. Then they were gone! Illusive, unobtrusive and non-invasive, they just vanished. His two adoring accomplices, astride his back; out of the castle. In the stables they pick up their horse and cart and storm into the fire that has taken hold of the heart of England. Onward to the warmth, safety and seclusion of Riche Mont. Never to be found, discovered, bothered. There for the length of their natural or unnatural lives. But together, the only company they all desired.

# HISTORICAL NOTE:

Joan, the daughter of Edward III and his wife, Philippa of Hainault, was betrothed to Peter of Castile, in 1345. He was the son of Alfonso XI of Castile and his wife, Maria of Portugal. In the Summer of 1348 the fleet carried Joan and her retinue from Portsmouth to Bordeaux. There they were received by the Mayor Raymond de Bisquale. He told them of the plague on their arrival. But they took no heed, just ignored him. They settled into the family castle overlooking the estuary of the Gironde. As her court began to die, she moved to the nearby village of Loremo. The princess herself finally died on the 1st July 1348. It was Andrew Ulford, who went back to England to inform her father of this sad occasion, in October 1348. By the 25th October 1348, the King had organised an expedition to Bordeaux to bring her body back home. But on landing at Bordeaux, there were no remains to gather. As the Mayor had set fire to the port, castle and surrounding area, in an attempt to stop the spread of the plague. Joan's' remains having been at the castle, when it had been burnt to the ground.